Amish Vows:

Amish
By Choice

By Rose Doss

Prequel

ISBN: 978-1-955945-53-0

Cover images courtesy of period images and canstockphoto
Cover by Joleene Naylor.

Manufactured/Produced in the United States

CHAPTER ONE

"This new *Englischer* friend of yours—Elizabeth—seems to feel privileged, like she has a right to all good things." James tapped the reins on the horse's back to start them moving, the late summer night still warm around them.

Sitting next to him on the buggy seat, Becky laughed, leaning over to bump his shoulder. "Bruder, you don't have to keep picking me up from the café after my shifts if seeing Lizzie *bothers* you. She's not so bad, you know."

Feeling a smile tugging at his mouth, he retorted. "It's all well and good that you serve food here, *Schweschder*, but you will not walk home such a long way and this Elizabeth friend of yours is nice to look at, anyway."

The steady *clumping* of Daisy's hooves filled the comfortable silence between them, the buggy reins a familiar weight in his hands.

Becky sighed contentedly, sitting back on the seat as they trotted homeward. "You are my favorite brother. It is a long walk back to the farm."

"I won't tell the other three *Bruders Gott* gave you that you said that," he commented in a dry voice.

"*Mmmm*, probably for the best," Becky grinned, "but then you're the only one who does things like worry enough about my walk home that you bring me to work and come pick me up after every shift."

1

"I hope your boss knows what a *gut* worker he's gotten." The horse's steps made a steady *clip-clopping* as other night noises swelled around them.

"Oh," her voice was breezy, "Mr. Milo is nice. He's a fair and reasonable *Mann*, not like my last boss at the dairy farm."

"I'm glad you're not working there anymore, even if we did get extra milk to make cheese." James clucked at Daisy to set her off again when they'd stopped to join a larger lane, passing by a newly-mown field with the scent of cut hay heavy in the air as they turned. "That dairy had crazy hours. Even when you work the early shift here, you don't have to be at the café in the middle of the night."

"Like I said," Becky grinned, "you are a very *gut Bruder*."

James lifted his brows, his mouth quirking to the side again. "I have to watch after you. *Mamm* and *Daed* have their hands full with the farm and the rest of the *familye,* particularly the younger ones."

"I thought you'd find my friend, Lizzie, pleasing to look at," Becky sent him a sly smile as she returned to his earlier comment. "Glad to hear you admit it. Others do, too, it seems. Just the other day, Mr. Milo teased her that several of our male diners come just to see her. A group of young *Englischer* men are there frequently and they look at Lizzie a lot."

James frowned. "You waitresses are hired to deliver food to the customers. I hope your boss doesn't usually comment on how his waitresses look…and I think you're very nice to look at, too."

"Oh, he doesn't usually say anything about that, but a really old *Englischer* happened to comment to him how pretty Lizzie is with her dark, dark hair and blue eyes. I guess it's not a usual combination, particularly around here. *Eldre* and *youngies* notice her."

"Maybe not," James glance over at his pretty sister. Her blonde hair neatly covered by her black *Kapp*, proclaiming her an unmarried Amish girl. "But I, myself, like lighter hair."

"If that's true, *Bruder,*" his sister retorted, "why do you find none of the lighter-haired *Maedels* around here attractive?"

"Who says I don't?"

"*Mamm*, for one. And you aren't courting anyone despite having returned from your *rumspringa* and joined the church."

James sat silent for a moment, the rustling sound of cicadas swelling around them as unwilling thoughts of Elizabeth's black hair and blue eyes sprang to his mind. "*Gott* will send me just the right *Frau*, Becky. Don't you and *Mamm* worry."

Looking out the café front windows two days later, Elizabeth noticed a black Amish buggy pull into the parking lot, registering that James—Becky's brawny, hunky and remarkably stoic brother—sat behind the buggy horse. This was Pennsylvania, after all, and Amish buggies weren't an uncommon sight, trotting down the streets as their owners conducted business.

It was probably a sin or something to find an Amish guy attractive, but James Lehman was hot, even though he never smiled. She needed to work on not noticing the breadth of his shoulders.

Carefully wiping the table under a front window, she ignored the accustomed chatter of the customers around her, frowning as she tried to see what had made Lizzie's stuck-up brother bend down next to another customer's car. Pushing the damp cloth in her hand over the table corners with an automatic swipe, she gazed at him intently. What the heck was that dark thing in his hand?

The man cradled to his chest whatever he'd picked up, seeming to speak to it. Then, as she watched in astonishment, Elizabeth saw a pair of tiny black kitten ears, stark against his white shirt as he strode toward the café door. Shadowed now by his broad straw hat, she couldn't read his expression, but it looked very much like James Lehman had picked up a stray kitten.

Intrigued, she looked toward the door as it swung open before him. Sure enough, cradled there in the man's broad hand was a small, scrawny, black kitten.

Elizabeth's mouth twitched at the sight. Over the last few weeks of working here in the café along with his sister, she'd grown accustomed to seeing James drop off and then pick Becky up after her shifts. He'd occasionally nodded at her, unsmiling, but she hadn't really interacted with him.

She was blessed to have found the café job and really fortunate to work with a new friend, like Becky.

Still staring at him, she was startled to see James beckon her over as he stood by the café door. Weaving her way between the tables, she stopped a foot in front of his big body. "Hi."

"Hello," he nodded. "You're Elizabeth, right?"

They'd met several times, but she supposed his experience was like that of so many other people—all those not like him looked alike.

"Yes, I am." She smiled at him and the kitten he clutched.

"Would you tell Rebecca that I'm waiting in the buggy for her?" He nodded to the scrap of fur in his hand. "The health code probably requires there to be no animals in the café."

She reached forward, scratching behind one kitty ear. "Hey, sweetheart. You look like you've been wet."

Elizabeth looked up to meet James' brown eyes. "I'll tell Becky where you are. Would you like me to bring you a towel to dry off the kitten?"

"*Yah.*" He nodded, his expression a little less forbidding. "That would be nice."

She gave him a friendly smile, refraining from telling him that 'nice' was her default. Not that he appeared to have noticed this. "No problem. I'll bring one out if you'll wait a moment by the door."

Ducking into the kitchen to grab him a rag to dry the kitten, Elizabeth reflected that James Lehman wasn't half-bad when he tried.

Elizabeth and Becky sat at a café table the next morning, having no customers for the moment. In the lull between the breakfast and lunch rushes, getting off their feet was nice.

"And you're telling me that James actually adopted that little kitty?" Her friend stared at her. "I thought he was the last man on earth to be susceptible to much of anything."

"Oh, he looks tough, but of all my *familye*, I think James would be the first to help anyone who needed it. He has a *Gott*-given kind heart." Becky blew on her cup of hot coffee.

"He sure looks tough," Elizabeth agreed from across the table.

"He's named her *Liebling*, which means 'sweetheart' or 'darling'." Becky couldn't help smiling at the thought. "James is really a terrific guy."

"Maybe," Elizabeth muttered, "but he looks like an Amish goon. That kitten-save was the first indication I've gotten of him having a heart, besides his picking you up after your shifts. That's certainly a gift from God. I don't know, maybe James is a great guy—to other Amish—and he just doesn't like me because I'm…what do you call me?"

"An *Englischer*." Becky's laughter gurgled in her throat, before she protested, "You just don't know James. He's very nice all around. I don't know why our girls aren't chasing after him. I mean they would be if he'd give them any encouragement. He says he doesn't like any of them. My *Mamm* prays all the time that he'll find the right *Frau* for him."

Becky shrugged. "I don't know. On the one hand, I want James to be happy, on the other hand, I can't really see him with any of the girls in the area."

"You two take a short rest," Milo called from the kitchen. "Then, we need to check the salt and pepper shakers to make sure they're full. Also, make sure every table is clean and that they're stocked with condiments."

"Yes, Milo!" Elizabeth sung out, not moving her feet from where they rested on the chair across from seat.

Becky nudged forward the little bowl of creamer packets. "Here."

Taking one to pour in her coffee cup, Elizabeth smiled at her friend. "You are the best, Becky. I'm so glad you came to work here."

"*Denki*." Her friend grinned before taking another sip of coffee. "I am, too. Otherwise, you'd have to handle all these customers on your own. Besides, working at the dairy farm was no fun."

Resting her chin on a hand propped on the table, Elizabeth yawned. "*Denki*. That's Amish for 'thank you, right?'"

Still swallowing her mouthful, Becky nodded.

"I don't know why I'm interested in the language. As far as I know, there aren't any Amish in California."

Settling her cup in the saucer, her friend squinted as she looked across at her. "Why, again, are you working your way to California? You don't have family there, do you?"

"Nope," Elizabeth lifted her chin to stare into space. "My only living family is my brother, Brandon. He's in grad school in Seattle and I may see him occasionally once I get to the West Coast. I don't know. He's a half-brother and a lot older. We've never been particularly close. Not estranged, you understand."

She shrugged. "Just not close like you and James."

"Then, what's in California?"

Elizabeth shook her head. "I don't know. Isn't that where everyone is supposed to want to move? At least, it is in the *Englischer* world. Maybe I'll find the perfect boyfriend there. Maybe I'll settle into the perfect job that turns out to be just what I want."

"I don't know," she said again, bringing her gaze down to meet Becky's.

Her friend glanced down at the Formica table top, her mouth pulling down in sadness. "It doesn't sound like you know what you want. I will pray for *Gott* to direct you."

"I'll tell you what I want," Elizabeth said in a low voice. "I want...I want some place to belong."

She looked across the table, a wry twist to her mouth. "You know, a place I fit in. Tell *Gott* to give me that. I've never really had it before."

"Hey, Brandon," Elizabeth spoke into her phone that evening, tired from her long shift, but unable to turn off her brain. "I'm glad I finally caught you at home."

Sitting on her bed in her efficiency apartment with one leg tucked under her, she lifted the corners of her mouth, hoping the smile somehow zipped through the phone connection.

"Hello, Lizzie." Her brother sounded tired or depressed. She didn't really know him well enough to tell, since he was older and had left home before they'd lived together long.

"How are classes going?" she asked in a cheerful voice after an awkward moment of silence, flopping back on the bed coverlet to look up at the stained ceiling.

"Okay, I guess. This engineering program is really tough, though."

Shuddering, Elizabeth said, "I can't even imagine liking math that well."

Her brother's laugh sounded perfunctory, like he heard that sentiment all day long and couldn't understand it. "Well, sometimes it's pretty tough."

A silence fell in the conversation and Elizabeth wondered if there was any point to this. Maybe she and Brandon just weren't meant to stay in touch. She'd even prayed about it and still didn't know if bothering to call him was worth her time. Her shifts at the café were long and she came home tired, but being cooped up here in her small place seemed lonely after chatting with people all day.

The quiet pushed in on her and she tried a different subject, asking her brother, "How do you like Seattle? Is it as pretty as they say?"

"Not knowing what you've heard, I can't say. It seems all right."

"Oh, I've only heard that the area is nice and not too hot."

"No," he said in his flat-tone, "it's not usually hot."

"I'm in Pennsylvania now," she offered in a chatty voice, smoothing her hand over the worn bed coverlet. "I'm waitressing in a café here till I get some money to get to Los Angeles."

"Oh?"

As interest went, his sounded pretty lukewarm, but she forged ahead. "Yes, it's nice here. We even get some Amish buggy people. I work with an Amish girl named Becky."

She could hear him swallowing. "That sounds interesting. Maybe you can learn something of their habits."

Reflecting to herself that it wasn't like studying the aborigines in Australia, Elizabeth couldn't think of anything to add on the subject. She'd always been a little clueless about how to engage her brother's interest, as their conversation confirmed. Now, that their mom was dead, they seemed to have little in common.

"The place I work is in a small town. Have you ever heard of Mannheim, Pennsylvania?"

"No, I haven't." He paused before asking in an awkward voice, "Is it a nice place?"

She wasn't sure whether he meant the café or the town, but she said, "Yes, the land around here is farm country and the hills roll on forever. It's really pretty."

"Well, good."

Elizabeth sighed. Brandon had never been less than kind, but he wasn't the most talkative guy, either.

"Listen," she said, accepting their conversation for what it was, "I'm sure you have homework or a test to cram for or something, so I'd better let you go."

"I don't cram," he said, a brainy, nerdy amusement in his statement. "It's not smart to wait till the last minute to study."

"Oh, right." Her four years at college seemed a life-time back, but she had no difficulty remembering having crammed before tests. Elizabeth doubted her English degree impressed him, particularly since it hadn't prepared her for any job in particular.

"Well, get back to studying—however you do that."

After she and her brother had made awkward goodbyes, she let drop the hand that had held her phone to her ear, her gaze again fixed on the roughly-textured ceiling. She hated this adrift feeling. The college friends she'd made had all wandered off to marriage and kids and grown up lives. It was foolish to think connections lasted through major life transitions. Laying there on the lumpy mattress, Elizabeth missed her mother more than ever.

When Colleen Thompson died in Elizabeth's nineteenth year, she'd felt bereft. Alone like she'd never before felt. That same feeling was still with her, only muted some in the past five years.

She liked having friends to help fill the empty spaces, but those friendships never seemed to stick any more than the relationships she'd had with boyfriends. She was smart enough not to fall into the baton-hand-off pattern to which many people resorted, one relationship to another, but she understood it. Being alone sucked.

Back when she was young, she'd gone to church with her mother and the peace of the place had always been remarkable to her. For some reason, the minister's words—and her mother's own quiet faith—had made a big impact on her. She'd always believed in God. Even though she'd never found her niche here on this Earth, the place where she belonged, she didn't doubt that there was one.

In the silence of her room now, she closed her eyes and sent up a prayer. The minister from her childhood had said that God's eye was on even the sparrow, but she'd always thought He had bigger things requiring his attention than her small self.

Still, she prayed.

God, thank you for your many blessings. For giving me life and leading me to this beautiful place. Thank you for Brandon. And for Becky and Milo. Amen

Sitting up, she leaned over to the stuffed bookshelf next to her bed, drawing from it a favorite book. She may not know what to say to her brother, but she had many blessings. She hadn't found her niche yet, but in the meantime, she could lose herself inside the pages of a novel and not feel so alone.

CHAPTER TWO

"Are you sure this is okay?" Elizabeth hissed a week later, sitting with Becky in the Lehman living room. "Your family doesn't mind you inviting me to supper?"

Becky patted her hand reassuringly before responding in an equally low tone. "Of course, it's okay, Lizzie. We're all happy to have you."

"James doesn't look all that happy," Elizabeth muttered under her breath. She felt like she stood out amongst the plainly-dressed Amish family, like a saloon girl amongst church goers.

It was a very simply-furnished house, several dark-colored chairs and two couches pointing toward a fireplace, and the whole place smelled yummy. The kitchen was situated at the end of the long-ish living area and Becky's mother, Lois, tended to readying the meal, assisted by her other daughters. Everyone—other than the taciturn James who had just come in—chattered away to one another, those helping in the kitchen occasionally calling out responses to things that had been said in the living area.

"You work with our Betsy at the café, yah?" Becky's father, Benjamin Lehman said cheerfully, his tone very like his daughter's.

Elizabeth returned his smile. "Yes, I do. It's been nice to have a friend at work."

"*Yah*. It is *gut*." Mr. Lehman nodded. "Becky has said the same, haven't you? You disliked working at the dairy with the people there."

Becky blushed, saying quickly, "I'm sure they're not bad people. We just had nothing in common."

"You mean they weren't of an age to sit around gossiping with you," her brother—Elizabeth thought he was Dan—commented in a teasing voice from where he sat on one of the couches.

"Supper is ready," Mrs. Lehman said, standing in front of the table. She sent Elizabeth an encouraging smile, "Won't you come sit down at the table?"

At her announcement, her offspring had risen from their various seats and gone over to find chairs around the table.

"There is an empty seat over there," she directed in a kind voice. "Right between Becky and James."

In the act of following her friend to a seat around the table, Elizabeth stopped, realizing who sat on the other side. Well, she mentally shrugged. Maybe she could get Betsy's quiet, kitten-loving brother to open up.

Sitting at one end of the long table, Mrs. Lehman bowed her head as her husband—situated at the other end of the table—said grace.

Her head bent during the prayer, Elizabeth smiled to herself at the cozy comfort of it all. A feeling of peace descended on her as Mr. Lehman offered thanks and prayed for their neighbors to prosper.

"We are not all here," Benjamin said once the prayer was offered, "Our oldest daughter, Abigail, is married to a *Mann* over Briarsville way and our son, John, just after her, has also recently moved. He bought himself a farm a ways from here."

"*Yah*," Becky's mother sent Elizabeth another nodding smile.

"There will just be the nine of us to supper tonight," Becky said, as if this was a small group. "*Mamm* and *Daed* and six of us children, plus you."

"That's a much bigger family than I'm used to," Elizabeth assured them, smiling at those seated around her at the table. "I grew up with only my mother and an older brother, who was out of the house almost before I knew him."

"James!" One of the Lehman brothers called from the end of the table as various dishes were passed along. "Did you ever get that cow out of the back pasture this afternoon? She wasn't cooperating when I saw you last."

With a broad smile that startled Elizabeth, James responded, "She certainly wasn't. I must have chased her three times around the pasture before I got her to go through the gate."

"Maybe she was playing with you, enjoying the chase," Becky teased from the other side of Elizabeth. Their chatter around the table rose and fell with James more relaxed and lively than Elizabeth had ever seen him.

"You saw him chasing that cow around and didn't go help?" Their dad asked the chiding question in a laughing tone. "Shame on you, Dan."

"I was too busy watching and laughing! It was so funny, watching a girl creature of any kind not respond to James!"

A shout of boisterous laughter erupted from the group and Elizabeth noted that James laughed, too, clearly not resenting his brother's teasing.

"*Yah*," he said, "the animal was having none of me."

"I'm telling you," Becky interjected. "She was enjoying having you chase her."

"Maybe that's the secret the girls around here need to learn," the youngest Lehman son suggested with a merry grin. "James must be directed to herd them and they should run."

"Hush," his brother responded, amusement in his voice, "have you no respect? We can't treat *Maedels* like animals."

From across the table, one of Becky's sisters said, "I think it's sad that you seem to like the cows better than any of the girls around here."

"Martha!" Mrs. Lehman said in a scandalized voice, a smile on her rosy cheeks. "We should change the subject. James doesn't need us to discuss this."

"Thank you, *Mamm*," he said, warmth in his voice as he smiled at her.

"If you're going to hang around us much," Becky joked to Elizabeth, "you'll have to get used to one of our *Eldre* telling us to change the subject every now and then."

"I would guess this subject might be embarrassing to James," Elizabeth agreed.

"Not at all," James said from his seat next to her. "My *familye* just likes to kid around and we all get used to being teased a little."

"Have you told Lizzie about your favorite chicken?" The unexpected question came from the other sister, a merry smile lighting up her face.

Elizabeth felt she was just piecing together everyone's identities, although they'd, of course, told her their names when she first arrived. All she knew was that Betsy had seven brothers and sisters and that one of each were missing from the gathering.

That and, of course, James. She knew James.

Just at that moment, looking down at the simple, homey table cloth, she saw his hand next to hers on the table, his larger and more tanned than hers, which looked girlishly frail next to his. Elizabeth swallowed, a flush of attraction startling her. She didn't even like James much. Well, she really didn't know him, not that that was particularly required for a tug of attraction to flare, she knew.

"By the way, James," Dan said, "where's the kitten?"

"Kitten?" he responded with a little frown, looking faintly irritated.

"Children," Lois Lehman chided. "You leave James alone."

Ignoring her gentle remark, Dan continued, "Yes, you know that sorry little black scrap you brought home the other day."

"I know where it is," Becky said, sending James a look of amusement that held a glimmer of understanding. "Asleep on his pillow, that's where."

"Cats make good mousers," he said in a flat, dismissive voice, a slight flush on his cheeks. "I'm sure you have no argument there."

"And we need mousers," his brother interjected. "In the barn with the livestock. Not so much in the *Haus*."

"Raven will live out in the barn when she's older." James glanced around, his gaze challenging.

His *Mamm* leaned over to pat his hand. "Don't let them tease you, der Suh."

"He's really named the kitten Liebling," Dan told the sister who sat next to him. "*Liebling*. Are you sure you will send her to the barn when she's older?"

"James has a gift with animals," Becky told her friend as her siblings joined in razzing the man to her left. "He's amazing with them."

"Particularly small animals," the younger Lehman brother added. "That chicken out back loves him and follows him around the yard."

"He even hugs the chicken," claimed their sister from across the table, chucking as she spoke.

"Hey, now," James shot back with a grin. "Bunny is our best layer, so hugging her is just my way of saying, 'thanks for the breakfast'."

The entire group erupted into laughter and the gathering was made noisier by several of the younger Lehmans calling out joking remarks to James about his devotion to this particular chicken.

"I can't believe he's even named her!"

"I can," Becky interposed as the noise dropped. She smiled at James across Elizabeth. "He's the kindest of us all, for all his forbidding face. He even names the pigs, don't you, James?"

Her brother smiled as she spoke. "Even pigs deserve *Gott's* love. You know, before they become food as *Gott* intended."

The family joshing washed over Elizabeth as their teasing back and forth continued, and she swallowed a profound longing. This is what she wanted. To be surrounded by a loving family. One whose values and beliefs matched hers. She was convinced she was meant to have been born into a large family and, yet, here she was, all on her own.

"I'm just saying," James repeated as he sat next to the fireplace with his *Daed* that evening, a small fire crackling there, "that I don't know what Elizabeth Thompson was doing here.

He had no reason for it, but the black-haired girl attracted his attention too much. She distracted him with her blue eyes, her beguiling smile and good-natured laugh. He didn't like noticing the *Englischer* so much…or noticing her very attractive shape.

"*Der Suh*, even she is a child of *Gott*," his *Daed* said in a mild voice. "She seemed like a nice enough *Maedel*, too. I'm glad Becky has more friendly folk at her work."

"*Yah*, she seems to like Elizabeth, that speaks well of her." James didn't know why he was hesitant to acknowledge anything good about her. It was unlike him to be unreasonable or unfair, but…she annoyed him and he couldn't identify why this was true. Generally, he shrugged off young women as they always seemed simpering and over-sweet. He'd liked to have found someone jolly like one of his sisters. Of course, there were girls in the church who were friendly enough, but thoughts of none of them stuck with him.

Maybe he'd have to travel to another Amish group to find a mate…or settle on a woman who would live the life *Gott* asked of all. The thought left him vaguely discontented, though. He wanted a *Frau* who loved him and whom he loved enough to join together as they faced this life. That didn't seem too much to ask. He wanted *Bopplis* that looked like the face that greeted him each day.

"It's just that Becky's friend knows nothing of our life."

"I think you might be unfair to this Elizabeth Thompson, James," his *Daed* pronounced after several minutes of comfortable quiet. "*Gott* tells us to love all. It isn't like you. *Gott* didn't say we should withhold that from those who haven't grown up in our faith."

"*Neh*." But Elizabeth Thompson with her long black hair and her skin-tight trousers probably wasn't what *Gott* had in mind, either, James reflected with a twist of his lips.

One Saturday night two weeks later, as he waited for his *Schweschder,* James unwillingly watched Elizabeth at work, as she balanced the stack of dirty plates in her hands.

"Excuse me," Becky's waitress friend said to an *Englischer Mann* at a table up front, smiling at him as she slipped several now-empty plates from the table in front of him. She turned to hurry back to the café kitchen where the clanking of dishes could be heard.

As Elizabeth's trim form sped past him, James drew in an irritated breath. He didn't want to even notice the *Englischer* woman. An Amish man had no business doing this.

Big, glass windows ran along the front of the café, dark now with the late night. Bussing tables wasn't really a waitress job, he knew from his sister, but there were several tables that still needed cleaning and James guessed Elizabeth was helping to finish the shift.

The place would be closing soon and, Becky had said no one left until all were through.

It would have been better, James thought, if Becky had never brought the *Englischer* woman to supper. Maybe he'd notice her less...although he had to admit that he'd registered her attractiveness before.

"Miss! Miss!" the *Englischer* at the front table called out with a beery smile.

Elizabeth reappeared with a dirty-dish tub balanced against her hip, stopping next to where the *Mann* sat.

He held up his empty mug, an appreciative leer on his drunken face. "One more for the road, pretty lady?"

Englischer behavior wasn't understandable to James.

To his disgust, he saw her smile politely in her friendly way at the *Mann* again, taking the empty mug.

"Of course, sir." She walked to the back, weaving her way through the tables back to get the *Mann* another beer.

James frowned at the table in front of him. Why did he even care if she felt the need to flirt with the *Menner* she served? The

16

woman was nothing to him, nothing, even if she was Becky's friend.

The room had gradually quietened as diners trickled out into the night and, now that several cars had roared off, he could actually hear the faint music that played in the background whenever the café was open for service.

Even with closing hour approaching, the staff had been scurrying around to serve a last surge of customers. Becky was in the kitchen, gathering a take-out order for an older couple who waited at a nearby table. The *Mann* who'd asked for a beer was the only other diner, lingering at what had previously been a crowded table near the front.

James sat at a back table to wait for his sister as he'd waited many times. It was even more important to drive her home after late shifts, particularly on weekends. Respectable Amish girls walking alone were sometimes harassed by *Englischers*.

From where she now wiped an empty table, the dirty dishes in a tub nearby, Elizabeth sent James a smile just then and, feeling heat crawl up his face at being caught staring at her, he found himself sheepishly smiling back. Doing so was only polite, he reminded himself. Why did he not notice the *Maedels* in the church this way?

It was then when she moved on to clear another table up front that he realized the male diner—whose table was next to where she worked—watched her with an almost-forbidding focus. The *Mann's* dark glassy stare roved over her form, although the café waitress uniforms weren't particularly provocative and had a skirt that ended at the knee, demure in *Englischer* terms.

Earlier James had become aware of the group at that table as they'd been loud and boisterous. He'd been watchful, worried that Becky served the group, but none had seemed drunk...then.

The others in the group had paid their bills and left several minutes before, but this man just sat drinking his beer.

"Hey, honey," he said to Elizabeth now, slurring his words. "How come you didn't serve us? Our waitress wore that long dress thing and even had her hair covered. You look real cute."

Crap. James blinked, watching Elizabeth and the drunk. He really didn't need this.

Englischer girls were used to this, he knew, but James found his body tensing, he sent up a prayer for *Gott* to help him not over-react.

Looking discomforted at this personal comment, Elizabeth gave the *Mann* a brief nod and a tight smile, before finishing loading the tub with dirty dishes and returning to the kitchen with these. James released the breath he'd been holding, glad the *Englischer* hadn't tried to block her.

Taking a deep breath—that he wouldn't even admit to himself was relieved the *Mann* hadn't done this—James meditatively rested his gaze on the *Mann*. Probably just a lost soul who had nowhere to go, the *Debiel*. The woman wasn't his business, after all.

This café had a pretty safe reputation, unlike the bar several streets over. He wouldn't have let his *Schweschder* work there.

Elizabeth stepped out of the kitchen again and walked through the dining room to finish cleaning the dirty tables, a damp towel in one hand and the dish tub in the other.

Telling himself that there was no actual danger, James still watched the *Mann*. He found his jaw firming as the *Englischer* again gaped at Elizabeth as she leaned forward to wipe the table. True, when she leaned forward, some of her creamy thigh was exposed, but not more than was acceptable in the *Englischer* world. It was certainly no reason for the *Mann* to gawk and leer at her like he was at some sort of indecent show.

As the man's focus grew more intent, James' jaw tightened and the tension slowly spread to include his whole body.

This situation wasn't gut. It wasn't gut for anyone. Elizabeth was no responsibility of his, but he couldn't watch any of *Gott's* children face harm.

As she moved past the *Englischer* to head back to the kitchen again, the *Mann* grabbed her, pulling the squirming woman onto his lap.

With a gasp, she pushed at his shoulders, saying in a tense voice, "Let me go, please! Let me go!"

Realizing he'd jumped to his feet, James' breath came faster as in an instant he took in the dismayed note in her voice. The glance he flashed back at the kitchen to see if Milo was witness to his employee's distress showed James that the café owner was nowhere in sight and the only two other customers in the place, an older couple, were watching the confrontation with dismayed, agitated expressions.

James abruptly strode forward, stopping several feet away from where Elizabeth still fought to free herself from the *Englischer's* grip.

"Let the woman go," he commanded more calmly than he felt.

Without expression, James took another step toward the *Mann's* seat where he held Elizabeth by the waist.

The drunk *Englischer* laughed. "Stay out of this. The girlie loves the attention, don't you, honey?"

He planted a smacking kiss on her cheek as she thrashed her head back and forth.

"No! Don't! Let me go!" Elizabeth panted, pushing against him in an attempt to free herself.

Gott did not wish them to hurt others on this Earth, but James knew he couldn't let her be molested this way. *Gott* would not want this. No woman should be forced to accept intimacies.

"Let her go," James said again, his feet planted firmly on the floor, his arms at his sides.

At this, the *Mann* lurched to his feet with an aggressive look on his face, sending Elizabeth stumbling back as he did so, held only from falling by the *Mann's* grip on her wrist. "And who's going to make me? You? You people don't fight, do you?"

Contemptuously not responding to this, James held his ground, reaching out to draw Elizabeth away from the *Mann's* grip.

Transferring his belligerent attention now to James, the *Englischer* said in a louder voice, "Do you want a fight? Do you?"

At that moment, out of the corner of his eye, James saw movement.

Still holding the *Mann's* glare, he didn't realize immediately what Elizabeth meant to do. Then, he registered that she was springing forward in a quick movement, Elizabeth heaved the contents of her dish-filled tub at the *Englisher*, crockery, globs of food, napkins and utensils flying everywhere.

The *Mann* sprang back, bellowing as food waste dripped off him.

The three stood in an angry, frozen confrontation, Milo, Becky and another kitchen helper erupting into the dining area.

"You bitch!" The *Englischer* screamed.

Broken plates and dishes littered the floor around the irate *Mann* who was splattered with food and dirty liquid. A limp lettuce leaf dangled over his shoulder and he stood glaring angrily at them, amid the broken crockery littering the floor.

"The girl did nothing more than defend herself from your attack," James defended her in a deadly calm voice. "Count yourself lucky she didn't have anything more dangerous to level at you."

"I didn't attack her. I was just teasing with her," the *Englischer* aggressively contended. "She had no call—"

"You grabbed her," the older male customer interjected with spirit.

"And you weren't letting her go," his wife added indignantly.

"I was just kidding around with her," the *Mann* declared, swinging back from them to James. "You saw her smile at me, didn't you? If that wasn't a come-on, I don't know what is."

"No, you don't." James didn't move, aware that after her brave moment, Elizabeth sheltered behind him.

At that point, Milo bustled forward, taking the *Englischer's* arm to urge him toward the door. "You can go now, mister! The café is closed for the night—and it's best if you eat elsewhere from now on."

"But I haven't paid my bill!" the *Mann* said in a belligerent voice as Milo shoved him toward the door.

"Never mind, never mind. It's on the house. Just go!"

Turning to stare at Elizabeth, James wondered if she knew just how unusual her action had been. Not satisfied with being rescued from the wolf, she'd helped fight back. She stood in front of him with her chest still heaving in agitation from the confrontation, a tendril of her black hair clinging to the side of her face, and as he looked into her wide blue eyes, he felt a stirring in his heart which he'd never before known.

It scared the tarnation out of him. Not her. Not this *Englischer* woman.

Glancing over to where Becky waited, like the others drawn out of the kitchen by the commotion, James said, "I'll be out in the buggy, Becky. Come out when you're ready to go."

With that, James turned and left the café.

He jogged down the restaurant's steps in the darkness and walked across the mostly-empty parking lot. The rustle and swell of katydid sounds filled the night air. The parking area was lit only by several floodlights at the café's corners and his buggy was parked in the farthest row. Struggling with himself all the way, he climbed onto his buggy seat and drew a deep breath.

Elizabeth was an *Englischer*. She didn't live by the *Ordnung* rules and any connection between the two of them wasn't healthy. Their worlds didn't mix and he needed to put all thoughts of her out of his head.

As he confirmed this reality to himself, the café door opened and he saw a woman in the café uniform come down the steps. His sister wore the café apron over her much-longer skirt. He didn't need to see the inky spill of dark hair to know this was Elizabeth. Jogging toward where his buggy waited, she came right up to him.

"James!"

Reflexively extending his hand to her as she mounted the buggy running board, he said, "Yes?"

She drew a deep breath, looking up and him and then leaned forward.

Before he had the presence to pull back—or even to knock his straw hat off—Elizabeth pressed her lips to his.

Everything inside of James went still. His dazed brain registered that she had the softest mouth, that she smelled good, even after working a long shift amid a bunch of food.

With her free hand, she held on to his shoulder, giving him more than a peck. Her slightly-open mouth pressed to his and, in a startled moment, he responded, kissing her back with a surge of response.

After a long moment, she pulled back, looking up at him with wide, startled eyes, and then Elizabeth smiled. "Thank you, James. Thank you for standing up for me. For that—and for the terrific kiss. Good night."

"*Goadenacht*," he responded in a slow, dazed voice as she scurried back into the café, an unsettling sense of trepidation seeping into him as he watched her go.

"And then I just kissed him!" Elizabeth laughed a little as she spoke to her friend. "You know, he was so wonderful with that drunk last night. James is a pretty good kisser!"

Picking up a tray of salt and pepper shakers from a counter across the room, Becky looked over her shoulder, frowning surprise on her pretty face. "You did what?"

Elizabeth couldn't help the smile that crossed her face as she shrugged, saying again. "I kissed James. He was such a sweetie, standing up for me that way."

She was accustomed to defending herself and she did it pretty well most of the time. Having James act to protect her had left her feeling mushy inside and their kiss in the parking lot had churned her up even more.

"That's funny," Becky said in an odd voice a few minutes later. "He said nothing of this to me when we drove home last night."

"It probably wasn't that big a thing to him." Elizabeth lifted her shoulder again, chuckling. "I hope you don't mind. I'm sure it was no big deal to him. He's probably used to rescuing thankful girls in distress. He probably gets a lot of chances, a powerful, strong dude like him."

Becky looked at her for a silent moment before saying, "No. James doesn't have much time for the *Maedels* we know."

"Well, he certainly helped me out last night. That big oaf was horrible."

Sitting the tray of shakers down at the table across from Elizabeth, Becky started filling them before looking up to say in that odd voice. "And James didn't say anything when you kissed him?"

"Nope," Elizabeth responded with a saucy smile, "and he's a really good kisser, too."

"You said that before," Becky responded mechanically. "It's just not… We don't usually go around kissing strangers, that's all."

In a lighthearted exasperation, Elizabeth reminded her friend, "Maybe not, but I'm not exactly a stranger, you know."

"You don't understand," Becky said after a moment. "You and James come from different worlds."

The restraint her normally-lighthearted friend's voice finally sunk in with Elizabeth.

With a frown she asked anxiously, "You don't think I offended him, do you? He was just being nice."

Becky sent her a smile, "I'm sure that was all it was. No, I'm sure he didn't think one way or the other of you kissing him."

"Good." Elizabeth looked down at the shaker she was filling, an unexpected pang hitting her in the midsection at her friend's words. She was probably being silly, but she suddenly wanted James to have enjoyed their kiss as much as she had.

.

CHAPTER THREE

The next day, after Becky had gone into the café to work, James was setting down a bucket of water where his buggy horse could reach it and he didn't immediately notice the smallish feet next to him. Running his hand down Harkin's broad, warm nose in a reflexive check of the horse's health, he became suddenly aware of Elizabeth next to him, her feet clad in sturdy black running shoes.

Glancing up quickly to her pretty, fair-skinned face, he looked down again, trying to erase the glimpse of her slender legs, visible in her short-skirted waitress outfit.

"Hello." Elizabeth gave him a friendly smile. "She seems like a nice horse.

Reaching out, she petted the horse's nose, cooing at it. "I think buggies are a lot more interesting than cars. Just think, you get to drive this sweetheart all the time."

James had never felt more awkward, like his hands and feet were too big when they'd just been regular-sized before.

"Harkin's a boy horse," was all he could find to say, cringing after he added, "He's a standardbred."

Like it mattered what this kind of buggy horse was called.

James had been raised to treat all their livestock well, as he would any piece of farm equipment. It just made sense. "He's a strong horse and easy to drive."

The whole moment was weird and he wished fiercely that he could stop remembering the feel of her lips beneath his. Their encounter with her drunken customer seemed to have sent everything sideways. She was just his *Schweschder's* co-worker, he reminded himself fiercely. He wasn't at all accustomed to feeling this awkward. Ever.

"Don't you," he scrubbed a hand over the horse's rough flank, "have to go inside for your shift?"

"In a minute," she agreed, scratching Harkin's ears.

"You were...good at defending yourself the other night," he offered abruptly because it seemed to need to be said.

"Aw, shucks," Elizabeth said, laughing again. "It's nice of you to say that, but I don't think I'd have had the courage if you weren't there to deal with him. All I did was throw a bunch of dirty dishes at him. You were great, though, the way you just stood there with menacing strength."

She was an *Englischer,* James reminded himself fiercely, trying to tamp down the glow her words triggered in his chest. They were not to involve themselves with those who lived worldly lives. "*Gott* does not wish us to...menace...our fellow man."

"Maybe not," she said with a chuckle, "but I don't think God would have approved of that goon grabbing me, either."

"Say," Elizabeth stroked a hand along the bonnet of his buggy, "I've never seen one of these close up. Can I look inside?"

"*Yah,*" he responded mechanically, thrown off balance by her enthusiastic interest in what was to him a mundane thing.

She opened the buggy door and stuck her head inside, "Oh, this is nice."

Determinedly averting his gaze, James still noticed the way her pale hand gently stroked the padded door lining. "My *Mamm* has body aches if she's jolted too much. The padded seats are mostly for her."

Elizabeth looked back at him with a coaxing expression on her face. "Could you take me for a short ride? Just around the parking lot and maybe that little loop in the street? I still have a few minutes before I have to report for my shift."

"I...suppose I could," he answered slowly.

"Wonderful!"

Before he knew it, Elizabeth had scrambled up, not inside the buggy, but onto the seat next to where he sat. Not knowing what else to do, he went around to the other side and climbed into his seat. A kind of windshield covered the passenger half of the front seat—in case of rain or chilly weather—while the driver had no glass in front of him to allow the buggy reins to run through to where the driver sat.

James took the worn leather reins in his hands, realizing for the first time just how close the seat was for two passengers. A flowery scent wafted from Elizabeth as he tapped the reins and he felt himself dying a little inside when all he wanted to do was turn and sniff her.

He didn't.

Since the horse's water bucket sat somewhat to the side, directing the animal around it wasn't difficult.

"Oh, my!" Elizabeth gripped the seat while bracing her other hand on the buggy dashboard in front of her. She laughed again. "This is faster than it seems! And the road is right there. No door or anything."

James grinned suddenly. "A door would make getting on the seat more difficult, don't you think?"

She chuckled. "Probably. Hey, this is fun! And you get to drive a buggy every day?"

"*Yah*," he responded tongue in cheek, "but you also have to feed the horse every day, not to mention mucking out its stall."

"Good point."

Her ready smile flashed and he noticed that her small hand had dropped from the dashboard and was now resting in a curl in her lap.

"But I still think it's fun." She turned to look out at the passing countryside.

"I'm glad," he glanced over at her, the corner of his mouth lifting in amusement at her simple enjoyment. She looked back in time to see his reaction, his grin drawing a widened smile from her.

Elizabeth tilted her head toward him. "Am I the first *Englischer* to ride in this buggy?"

The buggy horse trotted along.

"*Yah*," he answered at length. "Probably."

She looked at him steadily. "You don't mind, do you?"

James took a moment to think about this. "*Neh*. I guess not."

Elizabeth said nothing and then burst out, "Some do! Some Amish, I mean. Not your family, thank heaven, but there are others that come to the café sometimes."

He drew in a deep breath, considering how to respond to this. "You must understand that we, in our life, are directed by *Gott* to come apart from the world. We are, of course, directed to help our neighbors who may be in need."

"I wish my 'need' was visible," she said softly. "I'd like to have kindly interaction, you know."

James glanced at her curiously.

Her smile was fleeting. "I don't really have any family. I love that Becky has been my friend. My mother is dead and I've never known my biological father. My brother is older and…we don't have a lot of interaction."

The *clip clopping* of the horse's hooves filled the silence between them for a few minutes.

"You're welcome in our home." His tone wasn't particularly inviting and James hated that his rare moments of awkwardness made him less readable. "Whenever you want to visit with us."

"Thank you."

Her beautiful smile washed over him. James could feel the ripples of sensation over his skin as he kept his gaze steady on Harkin's ears.

"Hey," she said suddenly, "would you like to come to a fair with me? It's an *Englischer* thing, but you might find it interesting. There will be fried foods of all kinds and some games. I also think there are some other events, too. I promise not to expect you to violate your beliefs much."

By that time, James had pulled to a stop outside the café and Elizabeth was gathering her stuff in preparation to go in for her shift.

Gripped by an emotion he didn't fully understand, James put his hand on her arm as she was turning to get out of the buggy. When she looked back with a questioning lift to her eyebrows, he bent and kissed her.

Her lips were open in surprise at his move and, yet, after a frozen second, he felt her quivering response, registering in the back of his foggy mind that her hand rested on his shoulder.

27

Their kiss was both longer than it should have been and too short in his mind. When he drew back, noticing the rapid rise of her chest, he said, "*Yah*, Elizabeth. I'd like to go to the fair with you."

Her answering smile was both welcome and revealing.

She was no more immune to him than he to her.

"Good," she said, "I'm glad. Next weekend, then."

She got out of the buggy, looking back at him to say deliberately. "I like you, James. I really like you."

Watching as Elizabeth turned to trot into the café, he could only see dark waters ahead, but there was no denying that he liked her, too. A lot.

"*Please, Gott. Help me know what to do*" was James' fervent prayer.

"Who is that *Mann*?"

Elizabeth looked over at James in surprise, startled to hear an ominous note in his voice as he drew the buggy up under a tree in a shaded a corner of the fairground parking area a week later.

Knowing that he had no right to ask her about anyone in her life, she found herself answering him anyway.

"Who?" She said, craning her neck to look around the parking lot. The noise of the fair activities wafted out to them, a jumble of voices and snatches of music. Decorative flags fluttered from different booths and a carnival ride section could be seen off in the distance. The smell of different frying fair foods clouded the air like thick grease that coated the back of the tongue and her stomach growled embarrassingly.

"That *Mann* over there," James said steadily, pointing at the fair entrance. "The one who waved at you. Who is he?"

The buggy driver's seat, which she occupied next to him, required her and James to sit closely. The broad, stiff brim of his hat shadowed them and she felt the brush of his coat sleeve against her arm, sending a shiver through her. It was silly, actually. They came from very different worlds and this was just a day at the fair with a friend. There could be nothing more to it.

Although she was inclined to envy his large family...and to remember their kisses with heat in her stomach, she knew nothing could ever come of the attraction.

She was Becky's *Englischer* work friend. Period. Although, as far as Elizabeth knew, neither she nor James had mentioned inviting Becky along on this outing, or had even spoken to her about their day of playing hooky.

She didn't know what that meant and her thoughts shied away from even considering it.

Her hand on her stomach to quell any other awkward sounds, Elizabeth pulled her mouth down as she considered the young guy a moment. "I think his name is Craig. I've been trying to remember. He's a café customer. You've probably seen him there. He and his friends sit in the back corner."

Slowly, James said, "*Yah*. Maybe."

"They look like that bunch of college kids from the next town over," she volunteered. "You know, shiny cars and a privileged look?"

He laughed his short, dry laugh. "I thought all *Englischer's* had those."

She glanced over at the impassive face under his broad straw hat. "No, perhaps you don't know about the *Englischer* world. Suffice it to say, some have wealthy parents to pay for everything and some don't."

He glanced over at her with a warmer glimmer in his eyes. "I guess some have easier lives in this world than others."

"Yes, they do." She shrugged, thinking she'd have given up all of the college frat boy's money to have a family and lasting friends. "In this world."

The fairgrounds sprawled in front of where he'd parked the buggy—a leftover from another age in a parking lot filled with modern cars. She could see another buggy, however, on the far side and felt relieved, glad he wasn't the only Amish person present. She didn't want James to feel weird, although a swift glance at his impassive face made her wonder whether he had much reaction to the scene. Maybe she'd imagined the warmth in his eyes just now.

The guy baffled the heck out of her…and she still wanted him to kiss her again.

If he hadn't kissed her that way outside the café, she'd have thought she was crazy to imagine James had any reaction to her.

But he had and just the thought of being in his arms left her warm all over. With his broad shoulders and wonderful mouth, James was a real hottie, surely that was all this was.

"Well, come on," she said, scrambling down from the buggy. Today she'd worn her dark shorts and a t-shirt with her dark hair pulled back in a ponytail as the weather was pleasant.

In a daring move, she reached out and took his hand to tug him toward the fairground opening. "Come on! I think I need a buttered ear of corn."

James was surprised—and not displeased—when Elizabeth tugged at his hand to pull him forward. He laughed, allowing her to tow him along.

"Corn on the cob? Now? It's still morning," he protested, loving the twinkling smile she sent his way. "I'll watch you. I don't think I can eat corn-on-the-cob in the morning."

"Suit yourself, but it's really good any time of the day," she said over her shoulder.

All around them, booths were gaudy with flags and music jostled the sound of voices talking all at once. The place smelled of popcorn and beer and screams of joy could be heard from the rides area.

He even saw a sign-up sheet to play in the exhibition softball team posted on a board they passed.

As they walked further along the row of booths, the noise of it seemed to rise all around him and James was reminded of his other occasional other ventures into the *Englischer* world, only the fair seemed more of everything.

A little down the way, Elizabeth pointed to a large tent, saying "I think the beer garden is in there and I saw a poster that said there would be an arts and crafts show and competition, to award a blue ribbon to the best, plus a petting zoo and a floral show and competition."

"A flower competition? Flowers are *Gott's* glory, like rainbows…but *Englischers* compete with them?"

"Yes. Yah to you," she laughed. "It's just a silly thing, like the community softball game later. No one cares about winning. It's just fun."

"Sounds like quite a mix," he said, loving the warmth of Elizabeth's smaller, feminine hand in his. "What's that over there?"

James pointed to a roped off area across the clearing.

"The kids' area, I think. They have crafts and games for the youngsters. Oh, look! The food tent."

The smell of fried food was stronger as he allowed Elizabeth to drag him into a large striped tent where picnic tables occupied the bigger middle section and food was served by a loud, heavy-set *Mann* behind a cash register. When the *Mann* bellowed out orders to the open kitchen behind him, he sounded like James' *Onkle* Abraham.

Smiling, James ignored the curious stares cast his way as Elizabeth towed him toward an empty table. He absolutely knew he stood out amid the *Englischers*, although he wasn't the least bit uncomfortable with that.

Noting that there, at the end of the food line, stood the *Englischer* who had waved at Elizabeth earlier, James turned aside to find a seat at one of the tables.

The *Mann* was no concern of his and James knew he had no reason to be jealous of an *Englisher* woman, no matter how engaging she was. Although he felt some reassurance in the casual manner in which she now returned the *Mann's* wave, James tried to ignore this spurt of satisfaction her nonchalance gave him.

"There is the *Englischer* from the café," he commented, annoyed with himself for his need to point this out to her. She'd already responded to the youngie with that half-hearted wave.

"Yes."

She didn't seem all that interested to his great satisfaction. James berated himself silently. This was ridiculous. What if she did like the *Englischer*? She could be nothing to James. Marriage between believers and non-believers was a reason for excommunication and shunning. *Gott* had long warned them against being drawn into a sinful world.

"Are you sure you don't want anything?" Elizabeth asked in her engaging, enthusiastic style as she turned back to look at him. "I'm paying."

"Well, maybe I'll take a hot dog, after all…and I'll pay," he said after a moment. No reason to starve and the place smelled really *gut*.

"Great!" She beamed, taking the folded bill he held out. "I'll be right back."

It annoyed James that he noticed she didn't even say anything to the young *Englischer Mann* when her path to the serving area took her right by the *Mann* who looked her way.

In no time, she was back at their table. After she'd downed her corn—and him the delicious hot dog—they left the tent to wander along the row of open booths.

Off to one side, James saw the petting zoo area with baby goats and a pen of chicks at the front. In the distance, cattle could be heard mooing in a pen. When they came to a display of older tractors, James stopped. His and his *familye* fields were ploughed by hand, the horses pulling a plow while the farmer followed and directed the blade to create furrows.

Tractors were new-fangled and *Englischer*. James frowned at them. These, however, seemed much older than those he'd seen in use. He stopped as they passed the display of aging and rusty machinery, looking across the collection.

For a moment, Elizabeth said nothing. She then peeked up at his face, shadowed by the broad brim of his hat. "I think what can be accomplished by horse and man-power is amazing. You do so well with your plows."

With a dimpled grin, she added, "And you guys look so hot doing it."

James laughed, glancing over at her. "It's hot, sweaty work, most days."

"That's not what I meant by 'hot'!" She playfully punched at his bicep.

"Ow." He grimaced and made a big show of rubbing his arm as they moved on from the display, wandering along.

"I mean sexy-hot. You know. Our languages aren't that different."

"I've ploughed those fields" he said with grinning conviction as they walked past fair booths, "and I've seen quite a few others work their field. I've never seen a *Mann* look 'sexy-hot' doing it."

"Of course not," she said, walking next to him. "You wouldn't think another guy is sexy."

"No, but I also wouldn't want to make a *Maedel* plow fields."

She looked up at him. "A *Maedel* is a girl, right?"

"*Yah.* You're learning our Dutch, I see."

"I am," she laughed. "Becky has spoken some. She's been the best friend to me. I can't tell you. I'm so glad to work the café with her."

"You've been a gut friend to her, too."

"Thank you." Elizabeth beamed at him. "I think I've heard Becky say Denki?"

"*Yah.*"

She laughed, tucking her hand in his arm again as they turned to walk on.

At her touch, he looked over at her, glad they were together in this silly place, ignoring the inner niggling voice that told him he shouldn't care and certainly shouldn't enjoy this much the company of an *Englischer* woman. She drew him and he didn't understand why he never had these urges with any Amish *Maedels*.

"Hey! Look!" Elizabeth pointed at a carnival booth where what looked like old fashioned milk bottles stood in a row on a shelf. "There were games like that at the fair my mother took me to."

Flashing James a grin, she leaned closer to him to whisper in an exaggerated way, "She used to tell me she 'let' me win when we'd toss the rings, but I think she was just bad at it."

Drawing in a breath of her heady scent, he smiled back. "*Yah?*"

Perfume wasn't worn by the women of his plain life. He shouldn't have wanted to lean closer to her, but he did.

"Have you ever played the game?" She moved forward to the booth counter, tossing a glance at him over her shoulder. A man behind the counter—wearing a strange hat of stiff white foam—waited while she fished some money out of her purse, apparently to get rings to toss.

"*Neh.* I don't think so." He stood next to her, knowing that the elders and bishops in the church wouldn't be seen at a gathering so gaudy, no matter how simple and old-fashioned the games seemed. "It doesn't look so hard, though."

Elizabeth pulled a comical face. "You're just saying that because you've never tried it."

He reached his hand into a pocket and took out several dollars. "Then, let's play and see. Maybe you'll beat the socks off me. You go first."

Balancing a ring in her hand as if to test it, she looked back at him. "Are you sure you don't want to go first?"

Grinning as he pushed his forefinger up to tilt back the straw hat on his head, James said, "*Neh*, you go. I'll watch how you do it."

"Okay." She stood at the counter, leaning a little forward as she tossed her first ring with the flick of her wrist.

When it hit, but bounced off the corner of a bottle in the row, Elizabeth took another ring in her hand. The determined look on her face oddly made James want more to kiss her. The ring sailed through the air—and this one settled over a bottle neck.

"Very *gut*!" James praised, chuckling at her little celebratory jig.

"One down!" Elizabeth crowed, two rings still in her left hand. She took another and sent it flying toward the next bottle in the row.

It hit the bottle and seemed to waver, hanging on the top lip…before settling down around the bottle neck in a spiral motion. "Yes!!"

This time, she jumped up and down, wiggling her hips as she celebrated and James tore his gaze away from her movements with difficulty, pinning it on the ringed bottle.

"The fourth and last ring!" she boasted, holding it in her hand as she flexed it back and forth. "This is where I finish with a bang!"

"You did say this was your game," James said, loving how much fun she was having with this simple skill.

"Okay!" She tossed the remaining ring at the last bottle in the row and it went wide, disappearing behind the shelf a good three inches to the right of the bottle.

Making a sour face at the bottle, she turned back to say to him, "Your turn. If you get two rings on, it's a tie."

The man behind the counter moved forward to hand James four rings.

"Just toss them gently," Elizabeth instructed kindly, "and don't feel rushed. Throw it when you're ready."

"Okay." He eyed the row of milk bottles, glancing back and forth to measure the distance from the bottles to the counter. After a moment, he sent the first ring flying and watched it settle onto the neck of the bottle to the left.

"Good!" she said, "just like that!"

Holding up his second ring, James let it fly and was gratified to see this also settle around a milk bottle neck, next to the first."

This time, Elizabeth's encouragement was still enthusiastic. "Good! It's a tie. The bottles on the left are easier to get, though. Go ahead and try for the next one to the right."

James flexed his wrist again, letting the third ring fly...and settle around the neck of the third bottle on the shelf.

"Wow."

Without waiting—and almost hoping it skimmed over the shelf like her last one, he let fly the fourth ring. It just wasn't in him to deliberately lose, though, and he watched without expression as it also settled over the targeted bottle. All four bottles now had rings sitting on their necks.

"Well," Elizabeth said after a long moment. "It looks like you're a natural."

"You can pick a stuffed animal from this row," the man behind the counter said, holding up his cane to point to a row of pitifully-small bears.

"The purple one." The woman next to him didn't sound terribly excited. She turned toward him. "Unless you want another color."

"*Neh*. You can keep the toy. This game is a little like the Corn Hole game we play at Sings," James offered as they left the ring-toss booth.

She sent him a rueful smile. "Then, it's no wonder you're so good. I should have probably known you'd excel at something like that."

Not liking to see her downcast, James quickly said as they walked toward another game booth, "Let's try this one. You'll probably do better. It's some sort of water gun? I've never used one before."

"That's okay." Elizabeth laughed a little. "You don't have to feel bad about beating me."

"*Neh*, you show me how this one is done," James encouraged, taking her hand to tug her toward the game.

Laughing, she let him pull her over. "I'm not that good at water pistols."

"Well, you have to be better than me," he pointed out.

"I'm not so sure of that. You're probably good at it all."

"Just try," he said, handing money to the *Englischer* at this booth.

"This isn't necessary, James!" She watched him as he picked up a plastic water pistol.

"And we try to hit as many things on the red dots as possible?" He calmly asked the booth attendant.

"Yes, sir," the older *Mann* said, reaching out to point to the plastic part on the pistol that James was to pull. "Press the trigger back and the water will shoot out in a stream."

The water gun in his hand, James looked as Elizabeth with lifted eye brows. "I bet I hit more of them than you."

She gave a choking laugh and picked up the virulently green water pistol in front of her. "Okay, but you probably will."

Half an hour later, Elizabeth jigged along, chortling as they walked away from the booth. She clutched to her chest the stuffed animal she'd won.

"I can't believe out of all your choices, you picked that purple lizard thing," he commented with a smile as she pranced along beside him.

"It's a dragon, silly." She stretched out a piece of bright green section of fabric sewn to the lizard's side. "See? This is one of its wings. Don't tell me you've never seen a dragon before!"

He cocked an eyebrow at her. "Have you? Other than the lizard thing?"

"Lots of times." She waggled her eyebrows at him, her smile beaming at him. "It's an—an *Englischer* thing. Like the Easter Bunny and Santa's flying reindeer."

"I've seen a lot of deer in my time," James commented. "And none of them have flown."

"Never mind." She stuck the lizard under her arm, taking his arm again.

James registered to himself with the now-familiar pang that he liked her touch and wished to hold her smaller hand in his. That would be wrong, of course. Like so much of this day. *Gott, tell me what I should do with this longing for the woman.*

"Can you believe I won?" She shook her head. "I've never even used a pistol before, not a water pistol or a real one."

"You did very well." He knew that *Gott* sometimes chose not to answer prayers and that *Gott* had already been clear that His people needed to avoid temptation.

"Of course, you've never fired one, either. Are the Amish non-violent?" Her querying face was so innocent and sweet.

James struggled against a powerful urge to kiss her again. The act was, it seemed, habit forming.

"This is all fun," Elizabeth said. "Everyone will have a crazy day out here. The kids will compete in the mini hay bale toss and the coloring competitions and the farmers will drink too much beer in the beer garden, so their wives will have to drive home tonight."

"Mini hay bale toss?" he echoed as they came to the end of the row of booths. He saw now that the dirt avenue ended in front of a community softball field with warped wood bleachers behind the chain-link dugouts and a faded backstop that advertised some local hardware store.

"Yes," she confirmed, laughing, "there is also a grown-up hay bale toss."

"The throwers will have to be strong to toss regular bales," James commented absently, noting several *Menner* in the dugout, before he pointed to the softball field. "Did I see a sign advertising a community softball game?"

She glanced over. "Yep. I think so. Oh, look. That kid we talked about—Craig—and several of his friends are there."

James followed her to walk along the chain link backstop. They sat on the bottom row of seats on the bleachers, watching the group of young men, laughing and talking in the dugout. His jaw tightened. That *Mann*, Craig, who Elizabeth waved at...

"*Yah.*" He brooded at the softball field. "I suppose it's mainly going to be men who usually play here that will be playing in the softball game."

"Mmmm?" She glanced over at the group in the dugout. "I don't think so. It's not supposed to be a serious game. Milo said he might play, even though he doesn't usually."

"Milo?" James blinked at the mental image of Elizabeth's rotund boss playing…any sport—

"Yes." Elizabeth laughed. "Apparently, this game is going to be for all ages and all physiques. Milo is, um, used to sampling his own food."

He felt the side of his mouth kick up at the image.

"And Mr. Smithwright? The grandfather who brings in his little granddaughter for ice cream sundaes? He's signed up to play, too. I noticed his name on a sign-up sheet stapled to that light pole over there." She shook her head with a rueful smile.

"It's to be hoped that some younger *Menner* will play on Milo and Mr. Smithwright's team. The game can be fun for the fit."

She chuckled and James couldn't help, but laugh with her. "The other *Menner* and I sometimes played softball at Sings."

"Yes. Sings? Aren't those the youth gatherings Becky has talked about? Games like volleyball—"

"—and softball." He nodded.

"And then you all sing…church songs?"

James laughed. "Something like that."

"Hey, I have an idea!" she said suddenly. "You can play on Milo's team."

"What? No," James said quickly. "They all know one another."

"No, they don't. The game is open to all the fair goers and everyone here certainly doesn't know everyone here. I certainly don't think those college boys know anyone in town."

As he glanced at the young *Menner* in the dugout, James felt his jaw tense when the one named Craig winked at Elizabeth with a grin. He acted like she was here just to see him show off.

"What kind of games do you play at Sings?" she asked, tucking one leg under herself as she turned to face him more fully.

"Lots of different ones. Softball, basketball and volleyball. Hockey in the winter." He grinned at her. "Lawn croquet sometimes and corner ball."

"What in the world is corner ball?" She made a comically confused face. "I've never heard of that."

"Probably not. It's an old Pennsylvania Dutch game—sometimes played by the Mennonites, too."

"Well, geez." Elizabeth laughed. "It's amazing then that the games aren't on television."

James rested his elbow on the knee he propped up on the splintery bleachers. "Cornerball—or Eck ball, as it's also known—is a little like what *Englischers* call dodgeball. A smaller, hard ball is used and it's played on barnyards spread with hay for a softer landing. It involves a lot of jumping and spinning and diving to avoid getting hit. Mostly, *youngies* play the game, though, at school recess and such."

More fairgoers came to the field as they sat talking on the bleachers, the old wood planks trembling and shaking as others climbed to their seats.

On the softball field, James saw that teams were being formed and he couldn't help stiffening when the *Englischer*, Craig, came up to stand behind the fence right in front of them.

"Why didn't you tell me you were going to be here?" the young Englischer asked Elizabeth, acting like James wasn't there. "Me and my boys were planning to come to the fair. You could have come with us."

He gave her a big, cocky smile.

James noted that while Elizabeth sent him a moderate smile back, she casually reached out to again thread her arm through James', scooting closer to him as she said, "I'm here with James and we're having a great time."

The *Englischer's* smile dimmed and he nodded in a dismissive way toward James, his gaze returning to Elizabeth. "Well, we're going to hang out later at the Drunken Bug Bar in town. Want to come?"

"I'm not free, Craig. I'm here with James," she repeated, the polite friendliness fading off her face.

"Yeah, I know." He looked back at James, the flash of irritation in his eyes quickly shifting into meanness. "Hey, don't you Amish dudes play softball? I've seen some of you at the fields near our campus."

"*Yah*," James responded stoically, perversely wishing he had a straw to chew. The *Youngie* was annoying, but James quelled the urge to bait him, acutely aware of Elizabeth's softness pressed to his side, her light perfume rising to fill his lungs. It went against everything in which he believed. Fighting would earn neither of them anything, although the boy deserved to be taken down a notch or two.

The young *Englischer* glanced over at the dugout where his friends still waited. "Why don't you play? I think the teams are still forming. If you think you can play."

James met his challenging gaze, deliberately letting nothing show on his face.

"Go on. I think you ought to play," Elizabeth said suddenly.

He turned to look at her.

"Craig is being an ass," she said in a voice pitched for only James to hear.

"This is true, Elizabeth, but it is still no reason for me to play."

"No, it isn't," she agreed, "but the others are just playing the game to play—Milo and Mr. Smithwright. Play with them. Play for them. You can play on their side, not Craig's."

Staring at her for a contemplative moment, James considered this.

"Hey, buddy!" The *Englischer* Craig called out, smirking. "Play or not. We're gonna win, you know."

James could hear hooting and hollering from the one dugout, the other young *Menner* with Craig boisterous and loud, raucous in their contempt for the opposing team.

"Craig and his friends are jerks," Elizabeth said, pitching her words low, "and Milo's team will get beat to pieces unless they get some help."

"You think I can help?" He looked down at her with a faint smile.

She gave a jerky little laugh, caressing his upper arm. "Yes, James. I do."

In that moment, with the smell of the sandy softball field and the feel of the sun on his shoulders, he just knew he didn't want to let her down.

"Hey, ref!" yelled the young *Englischer* on the other side of the softball fence, "we have another player here, if that team needs someone."

Seeing Milo in the other dugout—waving now at James and Elizabeth—he knew he really wanted to help Milo's team win. From across the field, he could see that while he wasn't the only young Mann on the team, there were several others Milo's age.

Holding her gaze, he rose. "Here. Hold my hat. I will offer them whatever help I can."

James knew Elizabeth watched him walk down the fence to the dugout. Reaching the enclosure, he grasped Milo's outstretched hand.

"Hello, my boy!" The older man greeted him with a wide smile. "I was surprised to see you here with Lizzie. Are you playing with us? Will you be on our team? We could sure use you!"

"*Denki*," James responded, flashing a glance back to where Elizabeth sat on the splintery bleachers, beaming in their direction. "Although—why would you think that? You don't know that I've played before."

"No, I don't, although I've seen Amish boys playing sports, so it seems like a good guess." Milo's laugh was jovial. "You're also a fine, fit young man. Are you playing with us?"

For a second, it occurred to James that he just hoped he lived up to the older *Mann's* expectations. He never liked playing badly and, in this instance, playing with *Englischers* with Elizabeth watching, it could be doubly embarrassing.

"*Yah*," he said, "if you need more players. I wouldn't want to make anyone sit on the bench."

"Not at all." Milo clapped him on the back.

From behind home plate, a paunchy referee in stretchy sports shorts called, "Let's play ball!"

An hour later, Elizabeth clutched at his broad, straw hat as she watched James walk down the fence from the dugout after the softball game. Ducking her head in a brief prayer to ask for God's forgiveness for lusting after this beautifully-made man, she looked up, meeting his gaze with a beaming smile. Irreverent, admiring thoughts had lurked in her mind all while watching him very competently catch, hit and run.

Around her people milled, climbing down from the bleachers now that the game had finished.

Ignoring the voices of friends and relatives greeting one another and talking about the game play, she felt her heart pounding as James drew near. He'd played wonderfully and she found herself bouncing a little in excitement.

"You were terrific!"

James smiled, wiping his brow before he again donned the hat she handed him.

To the side, the young college guy named Craig could be seen leaving the dugout of the losing team.

Not wanting to be a sore winner, she smiled their way, nodding in a friendly manner. "Really. You guys crushed those boys! I loved the way you came back and won the game by several runs. Really terrific!"

James glanced down at her, a smile briefly creasing his cheek. "*Denki*."

"Your team beat the stuffing out of Craig's mouthy losers! I'm so glad!"

"I can see that. Although you seem very gracious." James grinned, clearly referring to her brief wave. "No one would know you think they're *mouthy losers*."

He walked beside her, his dark, plain coat over an arm, his lean, powerful body straight in his white shirt and Amish-style trousers. He looked as if he were completely unaware—or didn't care—that his garb, as much as his excellent play, made him stand out from everyone else there.

Elizabeth knew from Becky's comments that their mother and sisters made clothes for the family and she swallowed, conscious suddenly that she'd never before thought suspenders were sexy. She probably shouldn't think about them.

"It was close for a while," she said with a wide smile after a moment, "but I knew you guys could pull out a win! Do you usually play in the outfield? That one rolling-on-the-ground catch was amazing!"

"*Neh*, I should have caught that one more easily, but I misjudged where it would fall. And right field is the position players are usually assigned when others aren't sure if they're any gut at the game."

"Well, the team sure learned about you," she said, her blood feeling fizzier just walking next to him.

"Hey! Thanks for playing!" called a member of James' team, an older man with a small towel now draped around his neck as he walked past. The middle aged woman next to him, carrying his ball glove, beamed at them.

James lifted a hand to wave. "Thanks for having me."

"I don't think they could have won," Elizabeth said in a lowered voice, "if you hadn't gone out to help. You were wonderful."

He flashed her an amused look as they continued walking out, surrounded by other players and their families as they all streamed toward their cars.

Heading through the avenue of now-closing booths, the parking lot lay in front of them in no time. James' buggy was parked under a tree where the horse could lip grass.

"I'm so glad we came today," Elizabeth said, smiling up in his face as she leaned forward to bump his shoulder.

They stood next to the buggy on the passenger side, shielded from the larger parking lot.

She gave him a smile. "I've had a lot of fun."

He stood looking down into her face for a long moment, his expression unreadable.

Then before she realized his intent, James bent, kissing her very thoroughly. Elizabeth found herself clinging to his wide shoulders, the heated press of man sending her blood pounding.

When he lifted his mouth, she smiled tremulously. "I guess you had a lot of fun, too."

Later that evening, James quietly let himself into the silent *Haus*, carefully shutting the door behind himself. As the light was gone from the evening sky, he wasn't surprised to find the living room empty. Bedtime came early on a farm. Bending, he slipped off his shoes, carrying them as he quietly, cautiously walked across the planked floor.

When he rounded the bend in the staircase, however, he was startled to find Becky just sitting there in the dim light, her chin in her hand.

"Hello, *Bruder*." Her tone was low in the quiet building.

"Hello," he responded just as softly, eyeing her. "*Mamm*, *Daed* and everyone else has gone to bed?"

"*Yah*." Her voice was flat as she continued to meet his gaze.

"Then, why are you sitting here and not in bed also?"

"I was waiting for you," she said steadily.

"I told *Daed* I might be out all day and not come back till late." For some reason, James felt a tinge of heat across his cheekbones and was glad for the shadows. It wasn't as if he were caught in some misdeed.

"*Yah*, he told me."

"Okay, then, I'll see you at breakfast," he said, moving to the side to step around her as he headed on upstairs.

Before he'd moved up a step or two, however, Becky asked in a strangely calm voice, "Where have you been all day?"

James shut his eyes briefly. Here it came. Becky wasn't known for keeping her opinions to herself.

He looked back, hesitating for a long moment before responding deliberately, his voice steady, "I was at an *Englischer* fair. With Elizabeth."

Refusing to accept the shame he didn't feel at this choice, he just stared at her.

Becky rose to her feet from the step where she'd sat, saying jerkily as she did so, "I think you should take Hannah Schrock home from the next Sing."

"What? Why?" He frowned in irritated confusion at this response that had nothing to do with what he'd just admitted. "You know Hannah and I aren't courting."

"Well, perhaps you should be."

Noting the stiff set of her jaw and the tension in her body, he shifted around in the stairwell and they sank together to sit side-by-side on the narrow steps. Almost immediately, he felt the kitty, *Liebling*, at his side, pushing her small, furry head into his hand. He began petting her absently.

In a patient voice, he said, "We've grown up together—us and Hannah. It's not like I don't know her."

"*Yah*," his *Schweschder* said stubbornly.

"You know we have no interest in one another, Hannah and I."

"She could. Have interest, I mean. She might if she knew you had interest in her," Becky responded in a dogged voice.

"But I don't, *Schweschder*. I don't." His tone was gentle. "I don't have any more interest in Hannah than in the other *Maedels* here. You know that."

"Then you should travel to visit John or Abigail. Maybe you'll find your *Maedel* there. Others have traveled to different groups to find a *Frau*."

"Some may have, but not me. I don't think so, Becky."

"I think you would be happier in this life of ours, if you had a mate by your side." She cast him a sad, scared, upwards look. "I'm only thinking of you."

Slipping his arm around her narrow shoulders, James hugged her. "I know you want the best for me, *Schweschder*, but you must trust me to find this for myself."

Holding his gaze, Becky eventually dropped her gaze. "I do trust you, but I worry about you, James."

In all fairness, he could understand this and he couldn't, at this moment, say she had no reason.

"Hey, friend," Elizabeth said in a warm tone as, that next Monday, she sank into a seat at the café table opposite Becky. "I enjoyed having the whole weekend off. Milo should go visit his mother in Monksville more often."

"Yah, I'm sure she'd like that." Her friend didn't look up from the cup of coffee she was nursing and her tone was nothing like the bouncy, fun Becky she'd come to know.

"How was your weekend?" Elizabeth ventured on, hoping Becky was feeling well. "Was this a church Sunday? Did you all happen to meet at your house this time?"

"*Neh*, we met in Mr. Miller's barn last Sunday."

Becky hadn't met her gaze, still brooding at her coffee, the café silent and empty before opening.

"Are you feeling okay this morning?" Reaching across the table, Elizabeth patted her friend's hand.

Glancing up then, Becky frowned at her. "You took James to an *Englischer* fair this weekend?"

"Yes." After a moment—in which Becky continued to look down into her cup, her mouth turned down—Elizabeth asked, "Was he supposed to go with you or take you somewhere? I didn't know there was a conflict."

She blew across the hot liquid in her own cup.

"Lizzie, why are you after James?" The question burst out of his sister's mouth as she now glared at Elizabeth.

Putting her cup down, Elizabeth leaned forward to ask in confusion, "What do you mean?"

"*Yah*," Becky said in agitation, "James is a strong, fine *Mann*, but there are many others you can have."

"Probably not as many as you'd think," Elizabeth said with a laugh as she again extended her hand across to Becky. "But I'm not chasing your brother. Anyway, he doesn't strike me as an easily tempted guy."

Becky's hand turned to grip hers convulsively. "You must understand that we—we don't flirt and date as easily as *Englischers*. And an Amish *Mann* in our church cannot take an *Englischer* wife. He—he would be shunned. He would have to leave our life."

"Whoa, whoa!" Elizabeth lifted her hand from the table to make a "stop" motion. "No one is getting married here. And what do you mean 'shunned'? That sounds tremendously scary."

"It is." Her friend's face was solemn. "Shunning means that no Amish person will speak or interact with the—the wrongdoer. It as if the person no longer exists. If he or she continues to live in the home, all meals must be eaten separately, as well."

Becky shuddered.

Elizabeth felt her jaw drop as her friend went on.

"This is done to protect the blameless. To ensure that others are not tempted into ungodly ways." Becky looked up, her words becoming suddenly impassioned. "I do not want to lose James. Or to have him suffer the loss of all that he knows—his *familye* and his *Gott*."

While it was a relief to see her friend more like herself, Elizabeth could not reassure her fast enough. "Please. Please, don't be upset. I'm not...tempting James away from you and his family! I particularly wouldn't want to separate him from God."

She shook her head. "I wouldn't want to separate anyone from God. Please don't be upset, Becky."

Her friend stared at her, her face less cloudy.

"I know how much you love your brother. Believe me, I'm no threat." Her laugh was a little rusty, but she smiled as she chuckled. "It was just a county fair. No big deal. James was just being nice to me. I invited him without thinking."

"*Yah*?"

"*Yah*." Elizabeth reassured her with another smile. "Trust me. I'm not a danger to you…or to him."

"Why did you let that *Debiel* maul you?" James hissed in her ear a week later, having drawn Elizabeth into the short hallway by the café restrooms.

"What?" She looked up at him. "What's a diebell?"

"A *Debiel* is a moron," he said tersely. "You held him close just now! That *Englischer* from the softball game."

Giving him a long, irritated look, Elizabeth carefully detached her arm from James' grip. "What is the matter with you? Craig hugged me. I didn't hug him."

"You let him hug you! I saw you."

"Well, it's nice to know you're actually aware I'm in the same room!" She angrily turned to head back to the dining area, spitting out as she passed him, "You haven't even said hello or barely looked at me all week."

She'd meant everything she'd said to Becky about not trying to lure him from the Amish life, but it had eaten at her all week that James had practically acted like he didn't know her.

"He held you!" James said in a low, angry voice, following her out to the café dining room. "That spoiled *Englischer*!"

She whirled back around to face him. "Didn't you just come to get your sister? Well, she's off-shift now and you can leave!"

"I will," he called after her angrily. "You can be mauled by whomever all you want!"

Elizabeth watched him—his broad straw hand clenched in one hand—hustle a confused Becky out the door and across the parking lot to his buggy.

As she stood at a table to take an order near the front window, she saw them board the contraption and trot off.

"Did you get that?" the chubby blonde woman customer asked in a voice that said this wasn't the first time she'd asked the question.

"Oh! Yes." Elizabeth scribbled down on her order blank the order she'd heard with only half an ear. Repeating it back, she was absently relieved to have this confirmed.

Elizabeth then went back to the kitchen to put the order on Milo's rotating rack of orders, making herself ignore whatever happened outside the front window.

Later looking out at the café filled with diners, she barely noticed that Craig and his friends had left.

The scene with James kept replaying itself over and over in her brain. No matter how often she reminded herself that he'd been way out of line and had no business interfering in her life…she just kept remembering the strength of James' arms around her. The intoxicating press of his lips on hers.

The sound of his deep voice when he made some ironic comment.

She shouldn't care. Shouldn't think this way about him.

Standing in Milo's steamy kitchen, fragrant with onions and basil, Elizabeth shook her head suddenly, as if the movement would dislodge James from her brain.

Something needed to.

Closing the café door behind herself as Milo shut off the interior lights later that night, Elizabeth turned toward the lot to get into her car. Her steps faltered to a stop when she saw James' tall, broad frame leaning against her car door, his buggy parked at the back the lot. Pools of light splashed around the light poles studding the lot, casting shadows across his face and she drew a deep breath as she walked across to where he stood.

He looked intense, almost angry, but he didn't seem angry with her exactly. James wore no hat in the night air, his white shirt and suspenders outlining his upper body.

"I'm sorry," he said abruptly as she stopped feet away. "I was a *dumm hund*. I had no right to—to say anything."

Her tongue felt stiff in her mouth. "Thank you. Thank you, James."

Looking down at the asphalt pavement between them, he let several seconds tick by before he added, "I just had difficulty... It was hard to see..."

He looked up at her finally, saying with deliberation. "I didn't like seeing you in another *Mann's* arms."

Elizabeth didn't know what to say. His words sent a delicious shiver up her spine, but she knew this—whatever it was—between them was massively complicated. To put it mildly.

They stood looking at one another and in that exchange passed a wealth of longing and conflict. How could they know where this was going? What any of this meant?

"It feels..." Her words drifted to a halt. "I feel as if... James, this thing between us could...could burn its self out eventually."

He straightened from her car, stepping toward her. "Maybe. Maybe so, but I think we should find that out. Don't you?"

Elizabeth swallowed to keep from yelling her response. "Yes."

Almost before the word was out of her mouth, he'd moved to her, wrapping her in his arms. Held there, his heart beating strongly against her ear.

"I will pick you up from work tomorrow afternoon. Becky's not working and it will be just the two of us."

CHAPTER FOUR

"Tell me why you're here," James invited Elizabeth two days later as they ambled beside a mossy, burbling creek. Tall trees stretched up to form a lacy canopy overhead with spindlier green saplings brushing against their shoulders. Smaller bushes, clumps of fern and the occasional shade-flourishing wild flower framed the river path. The place smelled as beautiful and peaceful as the burbling water sounded and, even though it was summer, the air felt cooler here.

She sent him a dimpled smile, responding to his invitation, "Because you asked me to take a walk with you?"

"*Neh, Maedel*. You know what I mean." He let a smile lift a corner of his mouth.

A breeze shifted her longish, dark hair across her shoulder as they walked together along the creek, tugging at her soft knee-length skirt. The sparkling water shifted as the occasional shaft of sunlight broke through the trees overhead and James wondered again what it was about this girl.

"Yes, I do know," Elizabeth admitted with a chuckle. "You mean, here in Mannheim. Well, it's a long, long story."

"Too long?" He didn't know why this laughing slip of a girl had snuck into his brain as she had. He'd even found himself praying to *Gott* to take away this attraction he felt for her, to let him develop some draw toward a girl in the church.

Nothing.

"Beyond that you are Becky's friend and work with her at the café, I know little about you. Other than the fact that you don't hesitate to heave dirty dishes at an unruly customer and you haven't played much Corn Hole."

Her laugh rang out, seeming to fill the woodsy clearing. "Well, what else would a person need to know?"

"A thing or two more, I believe," he responded in a dry voice.

"Okay. Let's see," she mused. "*Umm*, the basics are probably best. I was born in Western New Jersey, not so far from here. I graduated from a four-year college with an English degree that's practically useless, unless I decide to teach, which I don't. And I'm an orphan."

"An orphan?" James looked over quickly, a sympathetic warmth stirring in him. "I'm sorry."

Elizabeth glanced at him with a smile before looking off toward the trees to the side. "It sounds so dramatic when I say it out loud. My mother died when I was in my junior year of college. She thankfully left me enough to finish school, but…"

Her voice drifted off, her beautiful face becoming sadder than he'd ever seen it. "But, I miss her every day. I thank God for her every day. I can only pray I'll someday be almost as wonderful a mother."

Sending him a brief, glimmering smile, she said, "Some kids never feel loved, but I always knew my mother really loved me. I think that's what I miss most, having someone to love me that much."

Walking along the river path beside her, he said nothing for several moments before asking, "What about your *Daed*? Is he also no longer with you?"

She shook her head with a rueful smile that held no self-pity. "My father was never with me. I don't even know who he is. My mother once told me they crossed paths when she was…having a rough period… Then when she found out about me, she didn't know how to find him. I have an older half-brother on my mother's side, though. Much older. He's my only sibling."

"Only the one?" James shrugged, before adding. "I know *Englischers* have smaller families, but yours sounds really small."

"Just us two and we have such an age difference, it's like being an only child. Brandon's in grad school in Washington State now. Philosophy, I think. Maybe computer programming?"

Elizabeth grinned before adding, "We've never been particularly close. We're not estranged, but he was pretty much out of the house before I was old enough to miss him and then he worked all the time before he ended up going back to school."

Reaching up to push aside a small sapling branch that tapped at her shoulder, she sent him another laughing smile. "So, you see I'm alone. I don't belong anywhere. Or with anyone."

"You have no *familye*?" James frowned at her, not knowing what that would be like. He'd always been surrounded by siblings and friends. "No *Onkles* or *Aentis*?"

"Not really. Mom had an older sister, but she died of emphysema when I was a little kid."

Elizabeth stretched her hand out to him for balance as she stepped across a narrow section in the creek. "Thank you!"

Keeping hold of her smaller hand, he easily followed her across the thin ripple of water. Stepping again onto the pebbly dirt beside the stream, James turned to head along the water, tucking Elizabeth's hand into the crook of his arm.

To his satisfaction, she didn't withdraw it, walking beside him. He couldn't deny the sliver of smile that crossed his face. James placed his hand over hers where it rested on his arm, responding to the glowing warmth this woman evoked in his chest.

I don't understand this, Gott, he sent up a flashing prayer. *Thank you for staying with me on this confusing path.*

"I envy you, James." She tilted her head to look up at him. "I really do. You… You belong here. You fit."

He considered this a moment. "I suppose. I have *Bruders* and *Schweschders* and cousins."

"And your farm," she added. "You have your farm here."

"*Neh*. It's a leased acreage, but I do alright." James added with a glimmer of a smile. "Larger families means our *Eldre* can't always provide farm land to us."

"I suppose not, but at least you have a family…and a place." Elizabeth stared at the creek. "I have neither."

She let out a long sigh before looking up at him with a bright smile. "That's why I'm headed to California. I'm just working at the café to earn enough to move on."

Glancing at her, James registered the beautiful curve of her cheek before he asked, "What's in California?"

"I'm not sure," she responded candidly, "but it's the place a lot of people want to go and I may meet my Prince Charming there. Settle down with him and have a family."

Looking over, Elizabeth added, "You know, find a place where I belong. Where I fit."

"Who's Prince Charming?"

She broke into laughter before saying, "Nobody. It's just a Disney reference. At least, I think it is."

With a rueful shake of his head, James said, "I don't know this Disney."

Laughing, she said, "No, but you're still better off here. You were born into the place where you belong. I'm still searching."

He looked down at the creek, aware of a thick cluster of tangled emotion in his chest, before saying, "I hope you find it, Elizabeth. The place where you belong."

Two weeks later, Elizabeth scooted her chair closer to Becky's in the crowded house and tried to look inconspicuous. She'd been surprised when her friend invited her to an Amish church meeting and figured this was Becky's not-so-subtle way of showing her how different James' life was from her own. As if she didn't know this already, she thought wistfully.

She liked him. Really liked him. She knew this wasn't good. It wasn't as if they shared a world, as if they could date in the regular sense, spending Saturdays at antique fairs and Saturday nights on her couch, watching movies and smooching.

It wasn't to be, she thought wistfully.

For a moment, Elizabeth let her thoughts wander to James' rare smile and the happy, safe sense she felt in his presence. She hadn't seen him here at the meeting yet, but she knew he had to be nearby. In the past several weeks, they'd met several times, always privately in some shady clearing or for an early evening buggy ride. Once, he'd pulled up next to a field of corn—one of his fields—walking together through the ripening stalks, while he talked of the principles of farming and the lifecycle of planting-growing-harvesting.

The worshipers around them began to quiet as an elderly man with a long gray beard and no mustache began speaking words she didn't understand. Becky had warned her that the service would be conducted in high German and that she wouldn't understand it. That didn't particularly matter to Elizabeth. Just being here and seeing how the Amish worshipped God was interesting. Over on the side of the gathering where Becky said the men sat—*Menner* she'd said—Elizabeth thought she recognized James' broad shoulders and short blond hair.

Reminding herself that she had no reason for her heart to pick up its tempo, she focused her attention on the preacher at the front of the gathering. This was clearly a close group of people. Everyone seemed to know everyone, chattering together in friendly voices.

All throughout the church service, she sat quietly next to her friend as the Germanic words of the man at the front rolled over her in what she knew were century-old sermons. There was permanence to it, the worshippers seeming intent and devout in their rituals. Elizabeth allowed the reverence in the gathering to sink into her, the peacefulness of it all making tears clog in her throat.

When she was a child, she'd gone to church with her mother, her simple mind liking Biblical promises of God's love. She'd always known He loved her, even when living in this world was hard. Even when her mom had died. He'd been with her even then, in her anger and pain. Over and over, Elizabeth reminded herself she wasn't alone, no matter how alone she felt.

It was just this world. This world seemed very lonely.

Becky's voice jarred her just then. "We all eat a meal now. Everyone."

Jolting out of her thoughts, Elizabeth realized the service was over and the worshippers around her getting up. Blinking, she said, "Lunch is a communal one?"

"*Yah*." Her friend nodded. "If that means we eat all together. There are women even now serving up platters of food. The children will eat first, of course. You see that tables are being set up?"

She did recognize then that the bustle around her had a purpose.

"Tonight," the younger girl said with excitement in her voice, "we will have a Sing. I told you about those, didn't I? All the young people come and we play team games—like volleyball or softball—before we all sing hymns together."

"Well, it is after all a 'sing'. It makes sense that there should be some singing." Elizabeth laughed.

"*Yah*, and we have all kinds of treats afterwards." Her friend's expression changed. "Of course, the real reason for Sings is to give *youngies* an opportunity to find those they want to court. The *Menner* often drive young girls home in their buggies. James usually takes one *Maedel* or another home."

"Does he?" Elizabeth kept her voice level, despite the stabbing sensation in her chest at the thought. "I'll bet you have lots of *Menner* who want to drive you home, too."

"A few," Becky admitted with a giggle. "But you will see all this tonight. I told you about the Sing this evening?"

"Oh, I don't think so," she shook her naked head. The Amish women—and girls, even babies—wore beautiful little caps on their heads. Black for the unmarried, Becky had told her, and white for those who were married. Her bare head was just another sign that she was an outsider here, too.

"You must come," her friend insisted. "Then you can see and meet all the *Maedels* and we can tell James which one to court."

Elizabeth abruptly got up from her chair. "I'm sure he can figure that out all by himself. Why don't we go see if they need help in the kitchen. Being so experienced, we can be the best servers."

Stepping out into the evening-cool air later that day, James paused a moment on the Miller's porch, the sound of cheerful voices inside the house fading. It had come as a surprise to him to see Elizabeth at the church gathering that morning and although she'd passed his seat with heaping platters of food several times during the lunch meal, they hadn't spoken. He hadn't been sure if Becky would bring her to the Sing that evening, but she'd shown up. All through the Sing they'd played softball and sang hymns and the others inside were now nibbling on desserts.

He and Elizabeth hadn't spoken beyond the brief social interchange expected of strangers, but he'd been acutely aware of her. All day. That morning at the service when they sat half way across the room from one another, at lunch when the swish of her skirt touched him as she passed by in her circuit to pass out the food. Now, this evening. His crazy sense of her registered when her laughter rang out during the games. He'd even picked out her voice from the others when they sang. Although she hadn't known most of the songs, she'd picked up on the verses and joined in.

The reality of how well she'd fit into this world made him ache. He wanted her so badly. If she'd been an Amish *Maedel*, he'd have jumped to court her.

Half an hour ago, when he glanced around the room for her, though, James saw Elizabeth was no longer there. He knew she'd driven her little car to their *Haus* to ride over here with Becky and it wasn't likely she'd have left.

Looking around the Miller yard now, she was nowhere to be seen. He jogged down the porch steps, feeling foolish as he glanced around the bushes in the yard. It wasn't like she was a five-year-old who would play at hiding in the yard. Not knowing where else to look as he judged it unlikely she'd go into the Miller's barn, he looked around the yard. It wasn't uncommon for courting couples to sneak out of Sings to canoodle in their buggies, but he'd not seen Elizabeth even talk to the other *Menner* there, much less get to a canoodling stage.

Besides, although not unfriendly toward her, everyone there knew the pretty, dark-haired girl was Becky's *Englischer* friend.

Not knowing where else to look, James walked slowly into the lower yard, where the Sing-attendees' buggies were parked. Several rows deep, the bonnets of the buggies were a dark spot in a darkening yard. He hadn't taken more than a step past the first row of buggies when he heard the unmistakable, but faint, sound of someone sobbing.

Brought up short initially, James eventually tracked down the soft noise to the last row of black buggies. At the far edge between the final buggy and a corn field with stalks that rustled in the evening breeze, he found Elizabeth.

Sitting on the ground by the rear buggy wheel, her dark head was bent forward, the sounds of her tears barely audible. If he hadn't been looking for her, he'd never have heard her.

James said nothing, merely squatting on the ground next to her.

She glanced up, her face pale in the dim light, traces of her tears visible on her cheeks.

"Why are you sad, *Maedel*?"

Not answering immediately, Elizabeth drew in a shuddery breath and looked down saying finally, "I just couldn't take it anymore."

He shifted to sit next to here. "Couldn't take what?"

When she didn't respond, James asked, feeling his brows snap together. "Was someone unkind to you here?"

"No," she said eventually. "No one was unkind."

"*Gut*. Because *Gott* has asked us to be kind to our neighbors."

Her face quivered and then crumpled again into tears as she sobbed out, "That's part of the problem, James!"

Hating her distress, he scooted closer, putting his arm around her shaking shoulders. "*Maedel*, do not go on crying. Nothing can be all that bad."

"Yes, James, it is!" Elizabeth insisted. "All this wonderful togetherness—your friends and family—everyone being so nice to everyone."

She shook her head, angrily swiping at a tear on her cheek.

Her words brought the twist of a smile to his face. "*Neh,* Not always. You just don't see it now, but we can be just as mean-spirited as the next, despite *Gott's* directions and His guidance that being *gut* to our neighbors is best for us."

"But that's just it!" Elizabeth shook her head again, sending the tumble of dark hair rippling over her shoulders. She looked up at him from the cradle of his arm around her. "That's just it. You, at least, have neighbors. People who know your name. Friends who will rejoice or cry with you when you need either."

She drew another broken breath, looking up at him with her beautiful, tear-stained face. "I don't have anyone or any place!"

Burying her head against his shoulder, she started crying in earnest and he barely made out, between her sobs, that spending the day with the church and joining in the Sing had brought all this home to her again.

His heart wrenching at her distress, James reached around to pull her against his chest. It seemed that if he could just shelter her there, he could somehow ease Elizabeth's deep sadness.

"You are not alone, *Leibling.*" The words spilled out of him fervently. "*Gott* loves you and you shine like the beautiful bluebells in the woods."

He reached down to tilt her face up. "Truly, you do."

Rocked in that moment, he knew that *Gott* didn't want him to turn away from her. Her distress and grief pulled at him. She looked up at him, her eyes dark blue and wet still with her tears...

And James bent to kiss her.

He'd kissed Elizabeth before—a lusty young *Mann* responding to a beautiful woman—but in this moment, his heart felt big enough to explode.

"*Der Suh,*" his *Daed* said when James got home that evening and stood brooding in front of the smoldering fire. "You seem troubled. What ails you?"

The rest if the family had gone up to bed already and the two of them were alone in the main area of the *Haus.*

James rolled his head back and to the side to stretch his neck.

His father waited quietly in the chair next to the hearth, seeming to know that James needed to collect his thoughts.

"*Daed*, I am—unable to forget, I'm aching for—for an *Englischer* woman." His statement was blunt, even to his own ears.

"*Yah*. How is this?"

As accustomed as he was to his *Daed's* calm responses, this still surprised a grin out of James before the gravity of the situation fell on him again.

"You know her. Becky's friend, Elizabeth."

His father nodded. "Oh, *yah*, her. A fine name Elizabeth. John, the Baptist's mother had that name."

"This Elizabeth works with Becky at the café. Remember? As I said, you and *Mamm* have met her several times."

"*Yah*, I know who she is." His father got up from the chair to come over and start banking the embers in the fireplace. "I believe she came to have dinner with us once and Becky brought her to church this very morning."

James sank onto a bench next to the fireplace. "That's her."

"A nice *Maedel*, I thought. And you…ache for her?"

"*Yah*, I do," he responded in a savage voice. "I do."

"I suppose you've had many chances to get to know her, since you take Becky to work and pick her up at the café."

His father's calm statement seemed almost ludicrous.

Leaning forward with his hands knitted into fists, James said, "I do. I know you and *Mamm* have always prayed we *Kinder* would live—"

"Plain and simple lives in the service of *Gott*," his Daed finished, nodding. "*Yah*, we have always prayed this."

"*Daed*," James's voice was low and steady, "I cannot stop thinking about Elizabeth. And I cannot envision a life without her."

"*Der Suh*," his father responded with a gentle smile after a moment, "you have never found amongst the *Maedels* in the church a woman who inspired a tenth of this feeling in you, have you?"

"*Neh*, I have not." James gave an even response.

"Then, you must sort this out somehow," his *Daed* said in his gentle voice as he put down the fireplace tools. "And you will. You are not a *Mann* given to decisions based only on your heart. I believe you can do this."

"Thank you, *Daed*," he said, watching his father turn and climb the stairs.

James sat alone then, embers smoldering safely under a blanket of ash in the fireplace.

He bent his head, murmuring, *Dear Gott, help me know what to do. I--care about—Elizabeth. I cannot stop thinking about her. Have you placed her in my life to help me understand Your love? Yet, this is a...mess, Gott. I don't what to do. Please help me.*

CHAPTER FIVE

"He was…wonderful." Elizabeth made a self-deprecating face at her boss, behind his grill. "I blubbered like an idiot. I wouldn't wonder if James wants nothing to do with me after that."

Dressed in his usual work attire of a short-sleeved white tee-shirt and jeans, over which was layered a now-smudged white apron, Milo flipped a sizzling burger with the practice of long ease. "Sounds like you had a girlie meltdown. My wife does it all the time."

Cocking her head to send him a steady look, she then sighed, saying in reluctant admission, "You're right. I did the girlie thing all over the place and James was great. He hugged me and told me everything would be alright. It was…great."

They were alone in the kitchen this afternoon, only a couple of tables out front occupied. One customer was already ploughing his way through a chef's salad while other the two waited for their orders. Since mid-afternoons were usually lighter times, Becky wasn't scheduled to come in for another hour.

Milo cleared his throat, looking over his shoulder at her in a needle-sharp gaze. "I wouldn't have expected an Amish boy to let an *Englischer* that close. Are you sure you know what you're doing?"

"I don't know what you mean." She smoothed the already-tight napkin around its utensils, a tray of already wrapped silverware in front of her. "Becky—and the Amish that I've met or served here—have always been very kind. They were even nice to me when I went to their meeting and the Sing afterwards."

"You haven't said whether or not you know what you're doing," her boss pointed out, scooping the burger off the grill with his metal spatula to lay it carefully on a bun.

Elizabeth swallowed. Milo was a good boss, but it wasn't as if she normally talked to him about her love life. If she hadn't been so conflicted and confused in her head now, she wouldn't have said anything today. Still, he never volunteered his opinions and never chattered about secrets. She felt she was safe to process a little with him.

"I saw James kiss you the other day." He scooted the bun onto a plate and then looked up at her. "Do you know what you're doing?"

Releasing a gusty sigh, she didn't say anything.

"You seemed to be kissing him just as enthusiastically."

"Where did you see us?" Elizabeth glanced over at him, her mouth drooping. "Do you think anyone else saw?"

"You mean Becky? No, she was inside serving and I'd stepped out to get a crate from the back. I don't think anyone else saw." Milo gave her a long, sharp look. "Do you love him?"

"I don't know what you mean." She picked up another napkin to wrap around a fork and knife, not sure herself of the answer to that question.

"I know you a little, Lizzie. Lots of girls that have worked for me dated a bunch of different guys. I can't tell you the number of kisses I've accidentally witnessed." He set the loaded plate in front of her, the customer's order complete. "This looked different. You seem different from that type a person. You've never dated around—that I've noticed—and James is Amish. We both know what that means. The two of you come from very different worlds."

"I know we do," she said the words in a low tone. "It's just that James—"

"He's a good looking kid." Milo interrupted as he turned back to his grill, starting to slather butter on two slices of bread that he then slapped on the grill to make a grilled cheese.

64

Rolling her neck again to stretch it, she said, "It's not that. I mean, not just that. He's… He's sweet and supportive and funny… And he seems to get me…"

"Two different worlds, chickie."

"I know. I know."

"I don't see how this can end well." Her boss slapped a layer of cheese on one piece of bread before flipping the other piece on top.

"Becky's upset with me. She's worried that I'll tempt James into a sinful *Englischer* life." Although they continued as before, Elizabeth felt the constraint in her friend's voice. She knew why she'd been invited to the church service the other day. Message received.

Tilting a sip of water into his mouth, Milo took a moment to swallow before he responded. "Maybe she's right. Maybe you could tempt him into leaving the farm."

"No." Elizabeth said emphatically, shaking her head. "James is—perfect—for his life. He loves his farm and his way of life. He fits here. I can't take it all away from him."

"Then, you'd better cut him loose," her boss said with brutal simplicity.

The words hit her chest with a sharp thump, the reality of what Milo said seeming to wrap crushing tentacles around her heart.

She blankly looked ahead. "I don't…know if I can."

"You've wiped that one plate for the last three minutes, *Bruder*. I think it's dry now."

Two days later, James stood at the sink, helping his favorite *Schweschder* wash up after the *familye* evening meal.

Stacking the dry plate in the cupboard, he took a dripping one from Becky's hand. Behind them as they stood at the sink, Andrew and Daniel sat in the living room having a lively, laughing conversation with Martha and Peter. Their *Mamm* sat knitting in front of the fire.

"Your mind is wandering," Becky commented when he didn't make any response to her observation.

"Maybe."

"Something seems to be weighing on you," she prodded, looking over in concern.

"*Yah.*"

"Can you not tell me about it?"

He shot her a quick look. "I don't think so."

"James," she hissed in a low voice, "what is going on with you?"

Not responding, he concentrated on drying the plate in his hands.

"Tell me." Her hands sank into the sudsy sink with the cup she'd been washing and she stared at him. "I can do this all day. I don't mind nagging you."

Knowing an irritable frown had descended onto his face, James said, "It's nothing. You don't need to worry. Nothing is going on with me."

Her hands beginning to again wash the cup, Becky stared ahead with a sad look on her face. "This is about Lizzie, isn't it?"

Putting the plate he'd been drying on the counter with a snap, he said, "I don't know what you're talking about."

"I'm talking about, dear *Bruder*, the fact that for the last week or so, you've come early to the café to pick me up—and that Lizzie disappears then."

"Don't be ridiculous," he recommended in a level voice.

"She disappears and then comes back in looking all dreamy and like she's been well-kissed." Becky hiccupped a small sob then, scrubbing fiercely at a cooking pot.

"Here." James said in a gentle voice, putting his hands over hers to stop her jerky movements in the dish water. He added with a dry humor, "What did that pot ever do to you?"

Becky let out a teary-eyed sigh. "James?"

"Here. Come out to the porch for a moment. No. The dishes will wait."

He led the way onto the railed-in area, lit now only by the yellow beams from the lanterns inside the house.

"*Schweschder*, do not cry." He hugged her.

She sniffled, saying, "Can you tell me, *Bruder*, that you've not been seeing Lizzie? That she is nothing to you?"

James released her, turning to stare into the darkened back pasture. His eyes wide open, he saw little, barely noticing the little glimmer of fireflies lighting up the evening. He couldn't lie to his sister. Ever since he'd drawn a weeping Elizabeth into his arms, his heart seemed to have left his chest. He could tell himself all he wanted that this was an *Englischer* girl who lived a different life from his, but it didn't make him stop thinking of her. Stop worrying about her. Stop wanting to show her that she did belong…with him.

Exhaling a gusty breath, he knew he couldn't imagine a life without her. Couldn't see himself with another *Frau*. He'd tried, really tried, to connect with the *Maedels* available to him, but he couldn't bring himself to think of any one of them once they were out of his sight. He couldn't stop thinking of Elizabeth, though.

He feared his heart had left him and gone into Elizabeth's keeping.

"I cannot tell you that she is nothing to me," he said to Becky. "You would not have me lie?"

"No, of course not."

Tears were coursing down her cheeks now and he saw this with a pang to his conscience. When Becky lifted a hand to wipe the wetness off her cheek, he brushed it aside, using the cuff of his rough work shirt to dry her tears. "Don't cry, Becky."

"How can I not when you—when you are considering a relationship with a woman that will end up with me losing you?"

When he didn't answer, she said sharply, "You know what it would mean? Shunning! I wouldn't be able to even speak to you. This is not your *rumspringa*. You have spent your time, considering what the *Englischer* world has to offer and you renounced it when you joined the church!"

James still said nothing.

"How can you not continue hearing *Gott's* voice and His direction to live this plain, simple life of worship?"

"I have prayed about this," James said finally. "And prayed. Asking His will over and over. I get no answer beyond this deep…belief. A solid warmth of love for Elizabeth filling me. I hear only this conviction that she is *Gott's* choice for me. The light of my life on this earth."

"How could it be that *Gott* would direct you into life other than what we know to be His will?" Her question ended in a soft cry.

"I do not know, *Schweschder*, but I truly love Elizabeth. She needs me and I cannot help but thinking of how alone she feels, that she has no one. She is a good-hearted, loving woman. A gentle spirit that hesitates even to strike back when pushed. Is this not *Gott's* way?"

"*Gott* does not want you to live in a way other than His will!" Becky insisted, the back window throwing a soft oblong of light over her stubborn face.

"He does not, either, wish me to walk away from my helpmate." James paused, not sure how to express in words the conviction that had grown stronger in him every day. "I am a better *Mann* with Elizabeth. A kinder *Mann*, less critical of others. More a reflection of *Gott's* love."

He reached out for Becky, hugging her again. "I know you love me, *Schweschder*, and that you want only the best for me. But…I believe a life with Elizabeth is best. She is my heart. I will always love her."

"James," Elizabeth said in a startled yelp the next morning, adjusting to two plates of breakfast in her hand as she shifted to the side of the kitchen passage to allow the bus boy to pass. "I thought you were coming later. Becky doesn't get off shift for several hours."

"I know." He tugged her back into the hallway toward the café back door.

"Deliver those real quick, so we can talk."

"Okay," she agreed over her shoulder, "but we sometimes get busy in the mornings."

None of this made any sense, but just seeing James made her heart skip.

After settling the omelet and pancakes down before her customers, she pointed out the shelf that held the bottles of ketchup, speeding back to the kitchen with a bouncy step.

"I'm back," she said, coming in to find James on a stool, watching Milo at the grill. "What's up?"

Slipping off the stool, James looked at Milo. "Can she take a break for a few minutes? We just need five maybe."

Her boss looked out at the Wednesday morning "crowd" which consisted this Wednesday of two tables of customers, both of whom were busily chowing down.

"Sure." Her boss looked at her, raising his brows as if to emphasize all they'd discussed only a few days ago.

Avoiding Milo's gaze, Elizabeth let James take her hand and tug her down the short hall and out the café back door. When it slammed behind them, James pulled her into his arms for a very satisfying kiss.

"I must talk to you," he said after kissing her senseless.

"Okay." She knew this could only end in heartache, but she craved time with James like her body craved air. Following him down the short ramp, when he asked which was her car, she answered without thinking. Truly, his kisses scrambled her brain.

"It's the little blue one over there. Wait, where is your buggy?"

"Never mind the buggy," he said, "Let's talk in your car."

"All right." She dug in the back pocket of her jeans, pulling out a key. "The door fob doesn't work anymore, so I have to unlock it with the key."

"*Yah*. Yes," he said, following her down the narrow parking area where employee cars were parked. In all, it was a good thing

Becky didn't drive a car because there wasn't much parking space back there.

"Here we are." Elizabeth stuck the key in the passenger door, smiling as she looked at him over her shoulder. "I'm glad you came early. I've been missing you."

As she trotted around to get in the driver's side of the car, she reflected that with his height and broad shoulders, James barely fit into her small car.

"Did you get the back pasture mowed?" she asked, taking his hand for no reason other than she loved holding it.

"Y-yes." He looked down at her smaller, fairer hand in his, muscular, calloused and tanned with his outdoor work. "But I did not come this morning to talk about farming."

She giggled, leaning forward to give him a kiss. "We can talk about anything, Gorgeous."

Smoothing his hand across hers, James said, "I have come to a decision, Elizabeth."

"You know," she confided, "I've always liked the way you say my name. Have I told you that?"

An answering smile coasted over his face. "No, but you can tell me things like that anytime."

"Thank you," she said with another laugh. "Now, tell me what decision you've come to."

"We have not talked about this much, you and I, but everything between us is complicated by our different worlds." He looked at her without expression.

Elizabeth drew in a long breath and let it out before saying, "I know."

"You came to dinner at our *Haus*, went to our church service and the Sing that evening. You've been Becky's friend since coming to work here."

Staring at him numbly, her gaze clung to his beautiful strong face and the dark column of his neck, the muscles in it shifting as he spoke. She'd known the end would have to come. He was breaking this off with her. She knew it. Milo was right. This—this couldn't help, but bring pain.

She'd have to quit working at the café. She couldn't imagine seeing him all the time, her heart freezing like an iceberg that calved off chunks of ice into the sea.

His hand tightened on hers. "We come from very different worlds. Your world has *Menner* like that foolish college boy I played softball against."

"Craig," she said, even her lips feeling numb as if she'd been shot through with Novocain.

"*Yah*, that *buwe*." James lifted her hand to press kisses on her knuckles. "You mean so much to me, Elizabeth."

This exchange was killing her and she wished he'd just do it already.

"I cannot—" He broke off, taking a breath before he went on. "I do not believe *Gott* wants me to live without you. You make me better in every way."

Elizabeth stared at him, unable to comprehend what he meant. "James?"

"This is it, my *Leibling*. I want to come with you, to stay with you in your world. This I can see…much more than I can see having nothing to do with you."

"In my world?"

His words made no sense to her—except the part about being better together than apart. With that, she completely agreed. "The *Englischer* world?"

"Yes."

Even his use of the positive *Englischer* term seemed specific to what he seemed to be saying.

"You'd leave the Amish world—your church, your family, everything? For me?"

"Yes, for us."

She'd dreamed her whole life of a man who'd be willing to do this kind of thing for her. Elizabeth stared at their griping hands, hers lighter and smaller, his dark from the sun.

"What about your livelihood? Your crops."

James shrugged. "Others will be glad to harvest them and keep what they gather for themselves. The major planting doesn't take

71

place until the fall anyway and, as the land is leased, there is no issue of selling the place."

"Then…what will you do? How will you find another kind of work?" She couldn't imagine James not working the fields. "You'll not work for *Englisch* farms?"

"I could, but I could also find work with others who have left the church. Some have woodcraft businesses." He bent forward over their clasped hands, kissing her again with thorough, slow deliberation. "You are my future, Elizabeth. My *Frau*. I have never found a woman I love like I love you. There are *Maedels* all around and I have tried to see a life with them. But I couldn't. Beyond the physical, carnal urges of this world, I cared nothing for anyone…until you. I'm asking you to marry me."

She started crying then, the irony of this horrible situation eating into her.

He pulled their interwoven hands toward his chest. "Do not cry, *Liebling*. Do not cry. You will never be alone again. You and I are together and will always work to serve *Gott* and make one another better."

In all her dreams, she'd never imagined loving a man as she loved James. Beyond his undeniable good looks, he had a heart as strong and pure as a man could have. Her brain in a scramble, she swallowed, sending up a silent, desperate prayer.

I cannot do this, God. Cannot let this man I love leave a life that fits him so well. Cannot let him give up his family, his livelihood and his church for me. Please help me be strong.

Her silent prayer seemed to summon a strength she knew was bigger than her own. Gently disentangling her hands from his, she said in a steady voice. "James, I'm sure Milo needs me inside now. Mornings are always busy. Let's talk about this later tonight. I'm off at four this afternoon. Can you meet me then?"

Looking a little disconcerted at her response, he paused a moment before responding, "Yes, of course. Where?"

Late that afternoon, James arrived some moments early at the spot Elizabeth designated, a quaint covered bridge, perched above the rushing river. He wasn't sure why, but uneasiness had crept between his shoulder blades all day. It made no sense to consider that maybe she didn't love him. Her kisses had been as warm, upon their separation her hug had been both tight and heartfelt.

It still niggled at him, though. He had no doubts about his course of action. He couldn't leave her. Not prone to sudden, rash action, he'd thought long and hard about it. Actions tended to occur to him suddenly, but that didn't mean he hadn't thought things out.

He'd walked to their meeting, not using the buggy as it was for many a symbol of the life he was now leaving. Sitting on the bridge parapet with the sound of the river running below, he reflected the irony that she'd chosen this spot. Aware that Pennsylvania was known for its covered bridges as much as for its Amish communities, he could only be glad no *Englischers* were there with their cameras. He supposed he'd no longer be of photographic interest and was glad of that, anyway, although not wearing his hat would take some getting used to.

This was a particularly beautiful spot, clusters of summer wildflower huddling at the base of several nearby rocks and tall, green-leafed trees rustling overhead. The graceful arch that provided crossing over the river was in good shape still, the builders having crafted a simple pattern of braces and cross-beams to protect the span over river. Focused on the simple beauty of the small wooden bridge, he didn't immediately notice Elizabeth's small, blue car pulling off the road nearby.

When he did look over, he saw her get out of the car, beams of sunlight highlighting her dark hair as it rippled over her shoulders.

James smiled. His Elizabeth was testament to *Gott's* great handiwork on this earth.

"I'm sorry to have kept you waiting," she said as she came toward him.

"I was early," he offered. "Was it busy at the café?"

"Yes, well, most of the day," she responded in a disjointed way, before pointing to a grassy spot off the road. "Let's go sit over here."

"Okay." Something in her manner had that uneasiness crawling between his shoulders again.

Once they'd both sat down next to one another on the green patch, she reached over and took his hand in hers. "This—this is really hard for me to say."

He knew her next words could be an expression that she didn't deserve him, but James suspected that wasn't what she struggled to communicate. She released his hand to pluck stalks from the grass under them.

"Just say it, Elizabeth. If you don't love me, you don't love me."

"It's not that." She abandoned her assault on the grass to nervously pleat the hem of her skirt. "This would be much, much easier if I didn't...love you."

"Then, tell me you don't."

Elizabeth looked up then and he saw that her beautiful blue eyes were flooded with tears. "I can't. I can't tell you that, but— James, I can't marry you. I should probably agree that I don't love you and send you on your way."

He frowned, saying in a level voice, "It sounds as if that's what you're about to do."

Shaking her head, she choked out, "Only partly. I won't lie to you. I have loved being with you. I love you, but it won't work."

"And I love you. What do you mean, it won't work?" James never understood before that a heart could crack and go on beating an empty rhythm. He'd heard of such things, but he hadn't understood them. To inflict this kind of pain, she couldn't love him.

"I can't. I just can't marry you."

"I don't understand. You tell me you love me, yet you cannot marry me?"

"No! I can't."

Her head bent as she sat next to him on the green patch, he saw that she was crying. In an angry, puzzled flash, he wondered if these were real tears.

James wondered if any of what he thought about her was true. Maybe everything he'd believed about her was a lie.

"We can't do this," she finally gasped out the words. "I can't marry you and take you away from—from everything you love."

"I love you," his voice sounding level and dead to his own ears. "How would marrying me take me away from you?"

She shook her head violently. "No! It would mean your family and your church would shun you. I can't take you away from all that. From your work on the farm. It won't work between us, James. You wouldn't be happy—"

"But you think I can be happy without you?" he heard himself demand in an angry voice, his hope of a happy life with her fading into bitterness.

"In time. In time, you will." Elizabeth took a deep breath. "I have to leave you here to live the life God intended. In time, you won't think of me any longer—"

"Do you really believe this?" he demanded with an irritated disbelief.

"Yes, I do!" she snapped. "I believe you'll find a woman—an Amish maydel—and you'll find yourself having feelings for her. You will live the life God built you for and I—well, I suppose I'll find my path eventually. I just can't allow you to leave your world for me. We wouldn't be happy."

James stood, looking down at her angrily. Getting to this decision had been very hard and she was throwing his love back in his face. "I think what you're saying, *Maedel*, is that you wouldn't be happy with me. You think marrying a *Mann* who was a simple Amish farmer doesn't seem like the best plan."

Scrambling to her feet, Elizabeth glared back at him. "I didn't say that. You're putting words in my mouth."

"If this is your answer," he spit the words out, ash in his mouth, "then you need to go find an *Englischer* that fits better."

"Thank you," Elizabeth said nervously a week later, wondering if she should have accepted Devlin's dinner invitation. A friend of Craig's, he seemed nice enough, although she wondered if he had different hopes for the evening's outcome than did she.

"Are you comfortable here?" Devlin asked her soliticiously. We can ask to be seated at a different table, if you prefer."

"No, this is fine." She forced a responding smile. The quiet, well-appointed restaurant reeked of upper-class privilege and Devlin seemed like a respectful enough guy—he just wasn't a broad-shouldered Amish man who made her heart flutter. She couldn't really blame him for that.

Allowing a waiter to place a napkin in her lap, she focused on putting aside her heartache and trying to enjoy the evening. She had to find a way to deal with this hole in her chest and the pointless longing for a man she knew she had no right to pull away from his life. Working with his sister would have been difficult and strange had Becky made any comment or acted at all like she knew what had happened. As it was, there had been no talk of Elizabeth's and James' interaction and no more invitations to church services.

"...so, a bunch of us decided to come here on summer break. You know, Craig's grandparents have a cottage near the lake." Devlin said, pausing briefly to give the waiter their orders.

"Anyway," he went on, his open face very different than the one of which she'd dreamed every night, "like I said, my major is finance and I should graduate next year."

She would have bet anything that his dad had a friend who had promised Devlin a job after graduation, but she didn't say this, just smiling as he chattered on. Driving here in Devlin's white late-model Lexus, they'd passed an Amish buggy with a driver in a broad-brimmed hat. Elizabeth couldn't help looking intently at the driver, but he hadn't been James. Then, she'd had to lie in response to Devlin's inquiry about her interest in the buggy, rambling on about her Amish café "co-worker."

She probably needed to move out of Pennsylvania, just so she'd not be triggered by every buggy.

As it was, she found herself hiding out in the kitchen whenever Becky was due to come on shift, her heart stuttering at the thought of seeing James. She knew he continued to drive Becky to work and pick her up after shifts. The reality of his nearness was just about killing Elizabeth.

Even her prayers to God for some reassurance that she'd done the right thing had gone unanswered. That was the thing with prayers. Sometimes, God said no. She just knew that He had a much bigger picture of everything than had she.

Sending up another prayer, she asked for His help with her rocky road.

Devlin chattered on and Elizabeth made appropriate responses, annoyed with herself for just wanting the evening to be over.

"So, how is it, working at that café? Good work environment? Good tips?" Devlin asked, lifting his glass to his mouth.

"Milo is a good boss and the food's pretty good." She stretched her lips into a smile.

"Well, maybe we should have lunch there one day this next week," he said with an almost childlike hope.

She started shaking her head almost immediately. "Oh. Oh, I don't think so. It's a nice enough café, but I'm there all the time."

Drawing a deep breath, Elizabeth realized she needed to move on. Needed to leave this town and find another place to live and work. Milo was great and she'd really enjoyed working with Becky, but she couldn't go on hoping to and dreading catching a glimpse of the man she loved.

James belonged here and she needed to find where she belonged.

CHAPTER SIX

A week later, Becky slid into the café booth where Elizabeth sat eating an egg salad sandwich in a desultory manner. Her friend looked at the bit of sandwich lying on Elizabeth's crumb-covered plate. "I'm sorry for interrupting your lunch break, but I have to talk with you."

"Okay." Weighed down with her grief, she could say no more.

"I have been wrestling with myself for days," Becky said, unnaturally somber, "but I have to speak."

She'd noticed that her chatty friend had grown more and more quiet. Elizabeth—caught up with her own misery—had wondered in passing if Milo had let slip that she'd given her two week notice, even though she'd asked him not to say anything. Milo was smart. He hadn't asked any questions, either about her leaving or her desire to keep this a secret from Becky.

After their conversation, Milo had to know what was up with her.

Now, Elizabeth crumpled the paper napkin in her hand, tossing it on the plate. "No interruption. I'm finished. What's up?"

Becky hung her head. "I'm sorry, Lizzie. I just couldn't help it, but—"

Looking up, she gave her friend a pleading, half-angry look. "I don't want James to leave, to move away and not be able to speak to any of us. Not to live in the way of *Gott*. I told him this…and I think he may have ended things with you because of me."

Elizabeth sat for a moment and then reached out a hand to rest it reassuringly on her friend's. "Becky, none of this is your fault. I know James is loved by you all, that his family needs him…and that he's happiest working the soil."

"*Yah*, he is happy doing that." She looked down at the table top and then at Elizabeth again. "But James is not happy now. Not on the farm or anywhere."

"What do you mean?" Elizabeth asked after a moment.

"Just that. James is not happy now. Not without you. And you—you are not happy without my brother."

Leaning forward toward the table, she opened her mouth to protest any interaction between them, abruptly closing it again.

"Good," Becky said with soft satisfaction. "It would do no good to lie about loving him."

"I—I'm nothing to your brother," Elizabeth protested. "I don't know what you think has been going on, but—"

"*Yah*, you are something to him. Do you think I haven't noticed you slipping out to see him when he came for me? Haven't noticed him being—I don't know—in a better mood all the time."

Elizabeth sank back against the booth, knowing her guilt showed on her too-expressive face. "Please understand—I never looked for this."

"You just met my James and fell in love with him," his sister concluded. "It's understandable. All the *Maedels* in our church have been half in love with him, too. Oh, for a long time, but he doesn't love any of them. He isn't happy around them like he is with you. If James had have given any one of those girls a second look, he'd have a *Frau* now. But he doesn't."

"He will, in time." Straightening, Elizabeth dusted her fingers with the crumpled napkin. "He'll eventually meet an Amish girl, settle down and start a family with her."

"*Neh*." Becky's face was sad. "Our *Eldre* thought the same thing—we all did—but James joined the church several years back. It would be time for him to take a wife, but he hasn't. He even refused when our *Eldre* offered to send him to another town where a good matchmaker resides. He said either the Lord brought him a woman to love or not."

Letting out a sigh, Elizabeth smiled sadly. "He'll find someone sooner or later. The right woman who'll bear him children and be by his side as he lives a—a plain, simple life."

"Maybe he already has."

"What do you mean?" Staring across the table, Elizabeth tried to swallow against the lump in her throat.

"Maybe you're that woman." Becky's words were flat, almost matter-of-fact like James'. "I have prayed about this and the conviction has come to me that James belongs with you, Lizzie."

"You're wrong." Elizabeth scooted to stand by the table, gathering up her dirty plate, tears prickling behind her eyes. "James needs to be with an Amish woman."

"I am not wrong that he loves you," Becky said with conviction, "and you clearly love him, too."

Later that afternoon, Elizabeth took a moment between customers to step out behind the café. Her vision was blurred by sudden tears and she gripped the landing railing.

Dear God, I know I must leave this place. I love James too much to interfere and make a mess of his life. I know I must leave now, not in two weeks. Help me, Lord. Help me.

Fishing her order pad out of her waitress apron, she leaned against the café wall to write a note to Milo. She hated to leave him in a breach, but Milo would understand. He'd find another waitress pretty quickly. He knew why she needed to leave.

She'd finish this last shift and leave the note on Milo's little desk in the back, telling him she wouldn't be back.

Scribbling this all on the back of several order sheets, she then folded these into a tight, little bundle. Shoving the bundle into one of her capacious pockets, she scrubbed at the tearstains on her cheeks and headed back inside to finish her shift.

The afternoon stretched on. Elizabeth's chest ached and she knew that—and the emptiness sensation inside her—was a reflection of her loss. She didn't think she'd ever feel whole again.

Just then, she caught a glimpse through the expansive café front window of James' buggy pulling into the café parking area.

Looking down at her watch, she realized it was later than she'd realized. Becky's shift ended soon.

Elizabeth drew in a sharp breath, her gaze fastened on James, his broad hat framing his strong features. She couldn't do this. Jerking suddenly on her apron strings, she yanked them free. Turning, she hurried to the back of the café. Tossing the apron on Milo's desk, she turned blindly for the rear door.

James tried to wipe the angry expression off his face and assume his usual blank expression as he went into the café to get Becky that afternoon. He'd considered waiting for her in the buggy, not wanting to see Elizabeth, but the very act seemed cowardly. Even though her rejection ate the insides out of him like a snake, he had to face it. Had to keep from holing up and hiding himself forever. That's what he wanted to do.

She didn't want him as her husband. He had to accept that. Beautiful, beautiful Elizabeth didn't want him.

Yanking open the café front door, he tried to banish this thought from his brain. A glance around the dining area showed Becky finishing with one customer while another waitress, who he'd seen a few times before, served a different table.

Elizabeth wasn't in sight.

Not seeing her was both a disappointment and relief. He'd dreamed about Elizabeth, although he'd never dreamed much before. Her dark, rippling hair. The sweet curve of her cheek… And her laughter. The warm sound of her laughter haunted him.

He'd felt drawn to her more than he'd ever felt with a woman, but she'd thrown off his offer of marriage as if he'd offered nothing.

"Hello." Milo, Becky's boss greeted James as the older man headed to the register at the café front counter.

"Hello." He eyed Milo.

"You look pretty bad," his sister's boss commented, throwing him a glance as he looked through the cash drawer.

"*Yah*." There was nothing else to be said.

"Did you come to get Becky?" Milo snapped the cash register shut, giving James a steady look. "Or are you here to see...someone else?"

"Becky," James almost snarled.

"Okay," Milo said, after a pause in which he continued to give James the same, steady look. "Wait here. She probably saw you come in, but I'll tell her."

Swallowing against the hard, choking sensation in his throat, James nodded and looked at the floor. He just wanted to collect his *Schweschder* and leave. This place had too many memories. Too much of a chance to see Elizabeth.

The chatter of the diners mixed in with the café faint music gave a background hum to the angry, sad thoughts tumbling through James' head as he stared out the front windows. He wondered if she was here and if not, where Elizabeth was, if she planned to now head to California to...to find a place to belong.

Even though she'd left a huge hole in his chest, James couldn't help hoping she found it. Her spot. Her right place.

Turning at the sound of steps behind him, he swung around to see Milo again. "Becky is coming right out."

"*Denki*," James threw out the word and moved to turn back toward the windows.

"*James?*"

He turned back to Milo.

"I should probably stay out of this," the older man said, "but..."

"*Yah?*" James knew he sounded less than friendly, but he couldn't help it at the moment.

"You should probably read this." Milo held out to him a piece of paper that was still wrinkled from having been folded.

"What?"

"Read it." Milo extended toward him the hand that held the paper. "Here. I think this might...help."

In puzzlement, James took the piece of paper and read what it said,

"Milo,

I can't finish this shift or the notice I gave you. I'm sorry. You were right about everything. We can't overcome everything between us, James and me. I have to leave. It's just too hard. I love James and I can't stand catching glimpses of him when he comes to pick up Becky—"

James' brows snapped angrily together, he flashed a glance up to see that Elizabeth's boss looked at him with compassionate eyes.

"Read the whole thing," the gray-haired man said, repeating. "It may help."

James blindly looked back down to the page, blinking so clear his gaze.

"...I've rejected James' proposal and his plan to leave his Amish family to live with me in my world. This can't be, Milo. He'd be so very unhappy. I can't stand that. I can't be the reason he's shut off from all his friends and family. Even his God. I must go, Milo. Please understand. I can't work the last few shifts. I love James so much."

"When did she give you this?" James asked in a thickened voice.

Milo leaned back against the counter behind the register. "This afternoon. Elizabeth was here earlier and then she left. I found this on my little desk in the back, along with her apron."

Looking up to meet the *Englischer's* eyes, he said sincerely, *"Denki.* For this. *Denki."*

"You're welcome." The man straightened from the counter as James turned away, still holding the paper. "I'll tell Becky you're waiting for her outside."

"Yes," James could hardly tear his gaze from the paper. *"Denki."*

Becky came out of the café not long after this, eyeing him as she climbed into the buggy. "*Denki, Bruder*. I know you had other things to do than come get me."

"It is no bother," he said, only half attending.

Directing the horse to turn out of the parking lot, James kept mulling over the situation in his mind. He hated the thought of Elizabeth alone. She had no one else and this wrenched at him. He couldn't help sending up pleas to *Gott* to help him, even though he knew his initial prayer had been heard.

Dear Gott,

What should I do? This woman and I belong together. I love her as I've never loved anyone and I now believe she loves me. She makes me a better Mann, Gott. A better servant for your message. But she's an Englischer. Help me. Help me know what to do."

When he got to the *Haus*, he let Becky off at the door to go in and help his other sisters and *Mamm* put together the evening meal while he trotted the horse and buggy to the barn out back. All the while, he brushed the horse, watering Harkin and giving the horse grain before he put the creature into a stall with a manger, leaving it lipping at the hay.

All the while, James brooded.

This could not be *Gott's* will, but he didn't know what to do. Elizabeth wouldn't accept his coming to join her.

Later, James sat at the noisy supper table with his *familye*, not attending to their chatter.

"Can you pass the mashed potatoes?" Becky asked, intruding on his abstraction.

"*Yah*," He handed her the bowl.

James knew *Gott* loved him and Elizabeth and that He knew the woman made James a better *Mann*. But how to fix this… How to bridge the gap between them?

In the act of receiving the bowl of mashed potatoes that Becky had handed back, the answer hit James between the eyes.

Holding the bowl in mid-air, he stared ahead in thunderstruck realization of his own density. Of course, *Gott* had answered his prayers. James had just been too slow to realize it.

He didn't know why he hadn't seen it before. *Gott* had all but branded it between his eyes.

"*Daed. Mamm*," James said, bolting up from his seat at the table. "I must go."

"Now," Becky inquired in confusion. "In the middle of supper? Where are you going?"

"*Yah*, now" he answered, halfway around the table, having tossed his napkin on his seat. "I must go now."

James knew he'd never remember jogging back to the barn. As he removed Harkin from the stall, hitching the horse again to the buggy, he reflected that *Englischers* didn't have to delay to do these things when in a hurry. They just got into their cars and drove off.

Then again, maybe the extra time to get his thoughts together was *gut*.

He didn't know if Elizabeth was still in her apartment or if she'd decided to seek comfort in the arms of another man. Despite *Gott's* direction that they should look at a person's heart, there was no denying that Elizabeth was a beautiful woman. She'd have no trouble finding a man to comfort her.

James climbed to the seat blindly, Elizabeth's note shoved into his shirt. Even if the *Ordnung* had directed them to wear fancier suits with pockets, having the sheet of paper close to his heart seemed more fitting.

She actually did love him. Her only reason for turning him down was that she wanted the very best for him. Elizabeth loved him so much she was leaving rather than have him make a choice she thought was bad for him. That was what she'd said in her note.

Without a doubt, James knew now what *Gott* directed him to do. He wasn't to stop living this directed life. He wasn't to be shunned and lose all contact with his family and his beloved Becky.

He didn't have to lose Elizabeth, either. If she'd just say yes.

Later that evening, Elizabeth got off the lumpy couch in her apartment, searching for a box of tissue to replace the one she'd emptied already, the evidence of her weeping left scattered over the couch cushions.

Scrounging her bedside table unsuccessfully, she grabbed several from a box she kept next to her makeup in the bathroom.

It made no sense to keep crying. She'd handled things herself for a long time...

In irritation, Elizabeth wiped at the new cascade of moisture on her cheeks.

Of course, she hadn't had to take care of herself without a heart before and there was no way she could reclaim that organ from the stoic Amish man who she loved too much. Many tears had leaked out of her eyes over the necessity to turn down his offer.

Pressing a tissue now against her damp cheeks, she was startled to hear a knock at her front door. Other than Becky and Milo, she had no real friends in this town. It was unlikely that Devlin would come by, given her lackluster response on their one date.

Before unbolting the door, Elizabeth looked through the grimy peephole. She hadn't lived alone all this time without learning to protect herself.

To her astonishment, James stood outside her door, the porch light yellow on his broad hat.

Her fingers numb, she scrambled to undo the chain and door latches. Pulling open the door, he stood before her in all his broad-shouldered glory. For a moment, she just stood there drinking him in, unconscious of the stained sweatpants she wore and the ravaged look of her face.

"Is Becky okay? Why are you here?"

A smile spread over his face and he ignored her questions. "I was worried you might not be here."

Wrapping the sides of her pilled cardigan over her chest, she said dumbly. "No, I'm here."

Her gaze clinging to him, she drew in a shuddery breath. "If— if you're here to repeat your offer, I have to tell you again—I can't. I can't take you away from your home."

"Are you alone?" James asked, glancing into the shabby living room without responding to her comment.

"Yes." She turned to gesture toward the empty couch, scattered over with clumps of used tissue.

Before she knew it, he'd stepped into the small room, saying, "*Gut*."

Elizabeth skittered back, not because she was afraid of him, but more out of caution. She shouldn't grab him and weep into his shoulder.

In the background, her small television burbled some commercial or another. All she could do was stand there, her gaze fastened on to him with a drowning intensity. He looked so good. So very good.

Standing inside her front door, James looked at her with more intensity than usual. "Elizabeth, you told me, when you rejected my proposal, that you loved me. Is that true? You love me?"

Throwing her chin up toward the ceiling, she squeezed her leaking eyes shut. "Is there a reason you're asking me this?"

She really couldn't stand this and the thought flashed through her mind that God shouldn't require her to do the noble thing again.

"Answer me," James insisted.

Opening her wet eyes, she glared at him, snapping out. "Yes. Yes, I do, dammit and no. You can't leave your church, your family and your farm to join me in the regular world."

James smiled at her words. "*Yah*? I can't?"

Blinking at the beautiful sight he made when he let his smile loose, she shook her head slowly.

"Then, I think we only have one choice, since we both love one another." He took a step forward and reached out to pull her into his arms.

"James, we shouldn't— We can't—" Her words were incoherent as she wrapped her arms around him.

"*Yah*, my *Frau*, we can." James enfolded her against his chest and tilted her head back of his kiss.

When he finally lifted from that very satisfactory endeavor, she blinked at him in confusion.

"I love you, Elizabeth, as I have never loved another woman. Come marry me and live in my world."

The magic of his arms around her drugging her, still dazed from his kiss, Elizabeth said, "What?"

"Come marry me, my *Frau*, and share this life of mine." His expression was tender and he bent to press a gentle kiss to the corner of her eye. "You don't need to leave this town or to keep searching for where you belong because you belong with me."

The thought dazzled her and she said through lips that were numb. "Can we—? Can a person just join the Amish life? Really?"

"If this is what you want." James lifted his eyebrows. "We can go to the bishop and, if you want, all this life offers. *Yah*."

"Wow." The possibility of actually sharing a life with him— even with all the hard work and the letting go of modern conveniences—hovered in front of her, an alluring possibility.

Maybe this was just exactly where she belonged.

"Then, yes. Yes!" Elizabeth burrowed against his shoulder. "Yes. *Yah*. I love you and I want this life with you."

Glossary of Amish Terms:

Aenti—Aunt
Bencil—silly child
Boppli—baby
Buwe—boy
Daed—dad
Bruder—Brother
Buwe—boy
Denki—Thank you
Debiel—moron
Der Suh—my son
Der Vedder—my father
Dochder—daughter
Dumm hund—dumb dog
Eldre—parents
Englischer—non-Amish
Frau—wife
Geschwischder—brothers and sisters
Goedemorgen—good morning or good day
Gott—God
Grank—sick
Grossdaddi—Grandfather
GrossMammi—Grandmother
Gut—good
Haus—house
Kapp—starched white cap married females wear, black if unmarried
Kinder—children
Kleinzoon—grandson
Lappich buwe—silly boy
Liebling—sweetheart, darling, honey
Maedel—girl
Mamm—mom
Mann—man
Menner—Men
Narrish—crazy

Neh—No

Nibling—one's siblings children

Onkle—uncle

Ordnung—the collection of regulations that govern Amish practices and behavior within a district

Rumspringa—literally "running around", used in reference to the period when Amish youth are given more freedom so that they can make an informed decision about being baptized into the Amish church.

Schaviut—rascal

Schlang—snake

Scholar—young, school-aged person

Schweschder—sister

Verrickt—crazy

Wunderbarr—wonderful

Yah—yes

Youngies—adolescents. Young people.

About the Author

Rose Doss is an award-winning romance author. She has written thirty-one romance novels. Her books have won numerous awards, including a final in the prestigious Romance Writers of America Golden Heart Award.

A frequent speaker at writers' groups and conferences, she has taught workshops on characterization and, creating and resolving conflict. She works full time as a therapist.

Her husband and she married when she was only nineteen and he was barely twenty-one, proving that early marriage can make it, but only if you're really lucky and very persistent. They went through college and grad school together. She not only loves him still, all these years later, and she still likes him—which she says is sometimes harder. They have two funny, intelligent and highly accomplished daughters and three granddaughters, whose names all start with E like their great-grandmother, Eloise.

Rose loves writing and hopes you enjoy reading her work.

Amish Romances:

Amish By Choice (Amish Vows Romance, Prequel)
Amish Renegade (Amish Vows Romance, Bk 1)
Amish Princess (Amish Vows Romance, Bk 2)
Amish Heartbreaker (Amish Vows Romance, Bk 3)
Amish Spinster (Amish Vows Romance, Bk 4)
Amish Prodigal (Amish Vows Romance, Bk 5)
Amish Rogue (Amish Vows Romance, Bk 6)

Becca's Boy (Amish Sisters Marry Romance, Bk 1)
Dinah's Darling (Amish Sisters Marry Romance, Bk 2)
Abigail's Admirer (Amish Sisters Marry Romance, Bk 3)

www.rosedoss.com
www.twitter.com - carolrose@carolrosebooks
https://www.facebook.com/carol.rose.author

www.ingramcontent.com/pod-product-compliance
Lightning Source LLC
Chambersburg PA
CBHW071234170626
46809CB00008BA/3057